D1289042

The Christmas Rose

A Rogues & Gentlemen Christmas Novella

By Emma V. Leech

****

Published by Emma V. Leech.

Copyright (c) Emma V. Leech 2020

Cover Art: Victoria Cooper

ISBN: 978-2-492133-22-0

Table of Contents

Chapter 1

"Wherein our hero is caught in the parson's mousetrap."

7th December 1820. London.

Felicity Bunting was five and twenty, and on the shelf. Everyone knew it.

Well, not any longer.

As of ten minutes ago, she had become spectacularly engaged to the wickedest rake in Christendom.

Suddenly, the dusty shelf she had resented for so long looked rather appealing, and she wanted to climb back on it and stay there, forgotten and unnoticed. For the first time in her life, the idea was positively blissful.

If she was honest with herself, Bunty wished she *had* organised this dreadful scheme, as everyone obviously believed. If she had been the mastermind behind this horrid scandal, at least she might have felt some sense of power, of having achieved her aim. Instead, she was mortified and ashamed, and wished she could curl herself up very small and hide in a corner… though the idea of buxom Felicity Bunting being able to appear small was laughable in itself. In a world where the ideal woman was slender, wraithlike, and prone to fainting, Bunty was tall, plump, and in excellent health. She bounced rather than drifted ethereally into a room, and would always prefer to laugh and have another slice of cake than sigh dramatically and appear mysterious and tragic. She was no Gothic heroine, yet somehow she had just made a tragedy of her own life.

And not just hers.

"It will be all right, Felicity," her mother told her, though her gaze darted frantically between Bunty's father and the unwillingly betrothed Lord Courtenay.

They had made a hasty exit from the party they'd been attending, only to discover the devilishly handsome lord on their doorstep five minutes later. Now, Mrs Bunting was huddled with her daughter on a loveseat, and Bunty thought her mama was trembling harder than she was.

"Though really, child, why on earth you had to make things worse by saying he wasn't the man you'd wanted to trap...."

"*Worse?*" Bunty repeated on breath of laughter. It had a slightly hysterical tinge to the sound, so she snapped her mouth shut for a moment before adding, "And that was not at all what I said. I said the trap had not been meant for him. I never said *I* set the trap, did I? I'm as much a victim of this as he is."

"Well, at least you'll be married, dear." Her mother's voice held a faint note of satisfaction at that, and Bunty stared at her in outrage. Mrs Bunting flushed. "I'm sure he's not really as bad as the scandal sheets make out," she added in a rush.

Bunty snorted. She had followed the wicked man's escapades for years now, and hadn't the slightest doubt he was far worse.

Her husband-to-be—she winced—Lord Courtenay, was speaking to her father on the other side of the room. He radiated tension, as well he might, having just been trapped into marriage.

Of course, everyone believed she had arranged it. Why would they not? She was five and twenty years old and had never received an offer of marriage. Not one. There *had* been Mr Arkwright, three years ago. He had seemed promising, but then someone had sniggered rather too loudly over the fact that Bunty was a full three inches taller than him and she'd never seen him again. Not that she'd been heartbroken, far from it, but still....

She didn't want to be a spinster, an old maid, a burden to her parents. Not that they would ever say as much, or even think it. For all they despaired of her, they loved her and wanted her to be happy. Well, so much for happiness. Oh, of all the men to trap into marriage, why had it turned out this way? Lord Courtenay, of all people. Just looking at him made her knees feel all trembly and weak. He was just so… large and vibrant and… *powerful.*

Well over six feet tall, he was perhaps one of the few men to whom she had ever stood close and not felt like an Amazon. He had thick, black hair, curled in unruly waves, and his skin was not the pale, insipid colour of most Englishmen in the winter months. Instead, it had a golden tint to it that only added to the impression of virile good health, and then there were his eyes. Lord Courtenay had eyes the blue of a Mediterranean sea, piercing and utterly swoon-worthy.

She sighed.

And now he would hate her until the end of time. Marvellous.

"Felicity," her father said, a look in his eyes that suggested he believed she had run mad. If he thought she'd deliberately tied herself in marriage to this devilish fellow, she could hardly blame him. "The arrangements have been made. You'll marry the day after tomorrow."

Bunty swallowed and dared a glance at Lord Courtenay. His face was a mask. Her heart quailed. Lord Courtenay—Ludo to his friends—had always smiled at her up until now. She had never tried to fool herself that his smile had any meaning to it, past a faint sense of pity and a naturally amiable temper—well, amiable towards women, anyway. Ludo was a rake of the first order, a hell-born babe, a troublemaker, and a black sheep. He was the youngest son of the Marquess of Farringdon who had thrown him out years ago, and Ludo had responded by putting all his energy into blackening the family name as far as he might.

He'd done a spectacular job so far.

Yet, unlike many of the men she had encountered, he had never been cruel. Not to her, anyway. There had been no smirking or murmured comments for her to overhear and make her blush with mortification. He had always given her that smile that caused her insides to quiver and made her feel muddled and giddy. They had not met that often, but for Bunty it had always been a memorable occasion. She had carefully packed away the thoughts of that sensuous mouth curving upwards just for her, to be taken out and relived again and again on the days when she felt alone, fat, and unloved.

Now he'd likely wish her to perdition on a daily basis and never smile at her again.

Oh, well. Such was her fate. As her mother said, at least she was getting married.

Bunty tried not to cry.

***

One hour earlier...

Lord Ludovic Courtenay, youngest son of the Marquess of Farringdon, was bored. This was usually cause for concern. When Ludo was bored, bad things happened. To be fair, Ludo did not *intend* for bad things to happen, not anymore. He had been trying his best to behave himself for over a year now, but he simply appeared to be a magnet for trouble. If there was something brewing within a mile of his person, he would gravitate—quite unknowingly—towards disaster. It was a gift of sorts, and one he was beginning to wish he did not possess. Once upon a time, he had revelled in his ability to create chaos and turn any polite party into a re-enactment of Sodom and Gomorrah, or Gentleman Jackson's boxing club. Recently, however, it had become a millstone around his neck. He was bored and tired and... lonely. Everything he had always enjoyed had lost any appeal. Brawling and causing trouble had long since failed to satisfy him. He supposed he must be getting old. A lowering thought. His ballet dancers and opera singers, and all the pretty ladybirds with whom he usually associated were lovely, and good company, and he was very fond of them, but….

But.

Ludo sighed and snatched a glass of champagne from a server. He ought not be here. This was not the kind of event he got invited to, which was why he'd had one of his less disreputable friends smuggle him in. The cream of the *ton* were here, and so he was not welcome. He'd be evicted at any moment, no doubt.

"Ludo, what the devil are you doing here?"

Ludo looked around to see the cool grey gaze of the Earl of Falmouth upon him.

"Falmouth," Ludo replied, smiling. "Don't worry, I'm on my best behaviour."

Falmouth snorted. His wife, the countess, gave a heavy sigh.

"Oh, *zhat* is a pity, and it is such a dull party, too," she said in her charming French accent.

Ludo grinned at her.

He liked the earl and his beautiful young wife. Unlike most others present, they were not the least bit stuffy. In fact, if the rumours about the earl were true, he was a dangerous man. Though close to two decades older than his wife, their marriage was a remarkable success. Tall, dark, and vigorous still, he was a striking figure, and his lovely French countess stared up at him as though he'd hung the moon for her alone. That the two of them adored each other was plain to see, and Ludo was struck by a jolt of something that felt remarkably like jealousy.

"Hunting, Ludo?" Falmouth queried.

"Hardly," Ludo lied, and felt an unaccustomed tinge of heat creep up the back of his neck.

The fellow was too astute for his own good. Ludo hadn't even admitted to himself that he'd come hoping to meet a nice young lady, and... and *what*? The usual experience was one of watching them blush and stammer and then remove themselves from his company as though the devil had come to tea. He supposed it was true enough. He had been so intent on punishing his family over the past years that he'd never stopped to consider he might be punishing himself, too. He'd made a career of showing his so-called father and brothers that he did not want them, just as they had spent his entire childhood vividly illustrated how badly they'd not wanted *him*, and now... well, now no one else wanted him either.

After a few words with Falmouth and his lady, Ludo moved on, draining his glass on the way and snatching up another. Two young ladies passed by, arm-in-arm, chattering merrily until they saw him. They blanched and skirted around him as if they might be ruined simply by breathing the same air. Irritated, Ludo winked at them and they gasped, hurrying away. He snorted. This was utterly pointless. He did not understand why he had bothered to come tonight.

Liar.

And there she was.

Felicity Bunting was standing talking to Thomas Tindall. Tommy, to his intimates, was the Earl of Stanthorpe, and an easy-going, good-natured chap. Under normal circumstances Ludo liked him, only... only he was making Miss Bunting laugh, and....

Ludo's chest grew tight.

It was ridiculous, really. He didn't know her at all, had never spoken a word to her. On the rare occasions they had crossed paths, though, he had admired her. There was something wholesome and real about her, as if she was truly who she appeared to be, with no pretence, no façade. Ludo had noticed she laughed often and with no restraint: a rich, joyous sound that made him want to smile. That was such a novelty of late he always gravitated towards her, as though turning towards the sun. She was also gorgeous. Thick brown hair and wide eyes of the same colour complemented a heart-shaped face with rosy cheeks that blushed a deeper shade at the slightest provocation. All of that without even considering the body that must lay beneath her gown, and God, did he want to consider it. She was all curves and softness, and he wanted very badly to seek comfort in her embrace.

So, why had he not approached her, demanded a little voice in his head. Because he was a bloody coward. *Him*, the wickedest rake in London, if the gossip sheets were to be believed, and he was terrified to approach a nice, gently bred lady in case she reacted the same way as all the others. He didn't want to see her look at him in horror, did not want to see her gasp and take a step back. Which was why he was still dithering here, watching Tommy enjoy her company whilst he stood like a dog outside a butcher's shop, salivating for something he could not have.

Yet, she had always returned his smiles. On the rare occasions they'd been in the same room, she had not looked quickly away. She had met his eyes and held his gaze, and she had smiled back. Every time. Ludo remembered every one of those occasions, from the very first, when his breath had caught in his throat in astonishment that such a woman should look at him with such open friendliness. That was where it had ended, though, for no one would dare introduce him to her. He'd all but begged on a couple of occasions, but with no joy. What kind of blaggard would introduce a man like him to such a lovely, innocent creature? Not one that Ludo had found. Though, perhaps Tommy....

Ludo moved forward. If he walked straight up to them, Tommy would feel obliged to make the introduction. The poor fellow was too good-natured to cut him. It was a rotten thing to do to such a nice chap, but needs must.

"Oh!"

Ludo stopped as someone ran into him.

"I beg your pardon," he said at once, though he was certain it had not been his fault. A woman gazed up at him in horror, a note clutched in her gloved hand. Was that one of the Ratched sisters? Ludo had reached out and taken her elbow to steady her, and now the woman appeared to be in shock. He let her go before she could scream blue murder. She was still staring at him, and still clutching the note. Ludo frowned.

"Is that for me?"

Her gaze darted wildly around the room. She looked as if she might be sick.

"Miss Ratched?" Ludo began, beginning to feel rather awkward. "The note. Was it meant—"

Before he could finish, she thrust the note towards him. Ludo took it from her, at which point she gave a little shriek and ran away. Good Lord! Did she think he would ravish her in full view of the blasted ballroom? Aggrieved, Ludo tore open the note and stared down at it with a frown.

Meet me in the library at ten o'clock. B x.

Ludo's breath caught.

B.

Felicity Bunting was known to her friends and family as Bunty.

Surely… Surely she wouldn't. He looked up, his gaze moving at once to where she was speaking to Tommy, and their eyes met. She smiled at him, a shy smile that made colour bloom on her cheeks, before she turned away again.

Hope rose in his chest. Ridiculous and foolish, for it was far more likely the B in question was a bored wife or a merry widow. There had been enough of those in the past to know it was the most obvious answer. Yet he wanted it to be Bunty, even as he knew he ought not go if it were. Ludo checked his watch. There was an age to wait yet, but he wanted to be sure he knew where to go, and that they were not observed. She was a nice young lady. Innocent.

If they were caught....

If they were caught, she would have to marry him.

He set down his glass and went in search of the library.

***

Bunty seethed with fury. She'd been having a perfectly nice evening—a miracle in itself—when she had taken herself off to the retiring room to freshen up. There, she had heard the Ratched sisters whispering together. The older sister, Jennifer, was already married. The younger, Sylvia, was not, which was something Sylvia intended to rectify this evening. Bunty was only astonished they were working together. The two of them were rivals in all things, and she thought Sylvia a fool to trust her sister to help her. That was neither here nor there, however. The fact was, they intended to trap Lord Stanthorpe into marriage, and Bunty would put a stop to it.

"A Christmas wedding," Sylvia said, giggling. "And he's as rich as Croesus, Jenny. Richer than your sweet William."

Bunty left, rushing from the room before they came out from behind the screens and saw her. She pushed her way through the crowd until she found Lord Stanthorpe again. He was right where she'd left him earlier, thank goodness.

"Tommy!" she said, grabbing his arm and towing him away from a conversation with Aubrey Russell. "Sorry," she added over her shoulder to Aubrey as she dragged Tommy across the room.

"Whatever has got you in such a pet?" Tommy asked, anxiety in his eyes.

"Oh, Tommy, the Ratched sisters have hatched a scheme. If you get a note from someone signed B, do *not* believe it is from that pretty Belinda Lovelace you were so taken with. It's a trap. If you go to the library, as the note suggests, you'll find Sylvia

Ratched waiting for you, and no doubt her sister and friends will burst in moments later."

Tommy blanched, the colour leaving his face so suddenly it might have been funny in other circumstances.

"Lud," he said faintly.

"Quite so," Bunty said, only too appalled by the vision of good-hearted Tommy married to such a shallow, mean-spirited creature as Sylvia Ratched. "So you must not go."

Tommy shook his head, his tumble of golden curls bouncing at the movement. "Indeed not. In fact, I'll go one better. Dull affair, at any rate. Was going to take Aubrey to my club."

"A splendid idea, Tommy."

"Don't need to tell me twice, Bunty, and I shall be on my guard from now on." He reached out and took her hand, shaking it vigorously. "Thank you, Miss Bunting. I shall never be able to repay you. *Never*."

Bunty smiled at him. "You're welcome, Tommy. Now, do run along."

She watched him hurry away and then turned. Bunty was not by nature a heroic creature, but such a vile scheme ought not only to be thwarted but exposed, even if she was the only witness. Taking a breath, she turned and headed towards the library, intending to give Miss Sylvia Ratched a piece of her mind.

Chapter 2

"Wherein misunderstandings and a hasty marriage."

7th December 1820. London.

Ludo had found the library with no trouble. It was well away from the ballroom, and an excellent location for a tryst. Now all he had to do was twiddle his thumbs until ten. Ridiculously, his palms were sweating, and his heart thudded in his chest. He was acting like a bloody schoolboy. But why? Why did Bunty want to meet him like this? *If it* was *Bunty*, murmured the voice of reason. He silenced it, wanting too badly to believe it was her and no one else. Likely it was the only way she thought they could meet. She must know as well as he did that no one would ever introduce him to her, and that smile, that sweet smile she had given him, surely a smile like that was a sign of encouragement? Wasn't it?

Finally, it was time. Ludo walked out of the ballroom, checking surreptitiously that he was not observed as he made his way to the library. He almost passed one of the Ratched sisters on the way. She was red-faced and looked furious, but did not see him, thank heavens. He lingered in a shadowed alcove as she rushed past. Ludo waited a moment longer, until he was certain no one was around, and then hurried on to the library, where he hesitated outside the door. *Please.* He sent up the prayer to a God he had largely ignored, and who had no reason to do him any favours, yet he opened the door and... there she was.

She swung around, her eyes growing wide as she stared at him.

The poor girl looked terrified. Likely she was having second thoughts about this mad scheme now. He could hardly blame her.

"Miss Bunting," he said, smiling and doing his best to look harmless. He closed the door behind him and moved into the room, noting that she moved the exact same distance away from him. "There's no need to be alarmed. I... I won't take advantage of the situation, you have my word. Only... I cannot pretend I wasn't surprised. Extremely pleased, but... surprised."

"S-Surprised?" she stammered, the word squeaked rather than spoken.

"By your note," he said gently. "The one that asked me to meet you here."

She gasped and grabbed hold of the chair she was standing beside, looking as if she might faint. "Oh, good heavens."

Ludo rushed towards her and slid his arm about her waist before she collapsed.

"What are you doing?" she asked, looking more astonished than alarmed.

"I was afraid you might swoon."

"I never swoon," she retorted indignantly, and then panic filled her eyes. "Oh, oh no. Oh, Lord Courtenay, you must leave—"

Before another word could be spoken, the door burst open and the Ratched sisters appeared, with what appeared to be half of the guests in tow.

"Oh, Miss Bunting!" Sylvia shrieked dramatically. "Oh, and with... with him of *all* men!"

Ludo jolted. Good God. It was a trap. Felicity Bunting had trapped him into marrying her! He waited for the anger to hit him, the outrage and fury at being so manoeuvred.

It never came.

All he could think was… *she wants me*. Not for just a night. Not just for a bit of bed sport. She wanted to *marry* him. Why, he had no idea. God knew he was no catch. He had no fortune, no prospects, so that could only mean one thing.

She wanted *him*.

His breath caught and he almost laughed as he turned back to look at her, wanting to tell her yes, yes, he would marry her happily. Yet she did not look the least bit triumphant about her victory. She looked pale and horrified.

"I'm so terribly sorry. It was supposed to be Tommy," she whispered, obviously mortified. "Not you."

***

Ludo knew this was undoubtedly the most miserable night of his entire life and, bearing in mind the quality of options on offer, that was saying something. He'd reached a new low, and no mistake. Not only had Miss Bunting not intended to trap him into marriage, but she would ruin herself rather than marry him at all.

Well, he'd damn well see about that.

Her parents had ushered her away from the party, and from him, before he could speak two words to them, but he lost no time in discovering their address and following them home. He would marry Felicity Bunting if it was the last thing he did. She had just ruined herself in front of the entire *ton*. She'd never get another offer. Like it or not, he was her best chance. Admittedly, that wasn't saying much, but it was the truth. He would give her the protection of his name and perhaps… perhaps in time….

He swallowed down the hope that rose in his chest and told himself not to be so bloody pitiful. Look where hope had gotten him this evening. He'd be a fool to expect anything good to come of this, except it already seemed he *was* a damned fool… for he wanted her too badly to let anything stand in his way.

Now, standing before her father in their front parlour, with Miss Bunting and her mother watching with frightened eyes from the other side of the room, he felt every bit the dastardly monster the *ton* had painted him. Not that he hadn't encouraged the rumours, but it was too late to lament.

He studied her as her father explained they would marry the day after tomorrow. She looked to be on the verge of tears and, despite everything, Ludo's heart went out to her. God alone knew what kind of man she believed him to be. She would have read the gossip sheets like everyone else; she would know of all his years of wickedness and vice. No doubt she thought she was marrying a vile fiend who would make her life a misery. Perhaps he *was* a vile fiend. He could not claim that all those stories had been untrue, for they each had some amount of truth in them, even if they'd been wildly exaggerated. Yet, he would try to be better. He would try to be a good man. Once Ludo had explained his situation, Miss Bunting's father had made no bones about his displeasure, pointing out that his daughter was getting a bad bargain indeed, but Ludo had spent the last year clearing his debts and trying to get his finances in order. He was in no position to provide for a wife, but he would try. He would find a way to give her a home. A home. The idea called to some place deep inside him he had buried years ago. He had not known what it was to have a home. Not since his mother had died, at least.

Miss Bunting had a reasonable dowry, more than anything he might have expected to gain through marriage, considering his prospects, but the idea of living off her money made his stomach clench, and shame rose in him like a tide. He would be better than that.

"Papa, do you think we might have a few moments alone together, please?"

Ludo looked up in surprise as he realised Miss Bunting had made the request. How brave she was. She was miserable and afraid, but she would not shy away from him. Thank God for that.

Her father looked none too happy about it.

"Mr Bunting," Ludo said, somewhat testy now. He was the one who'd been trapped, after all. "We shall soon be married, and I promise to act the gentleman. I do have a vague recollection of how to do so."

Mr Bunting gave him a dark look filled with mistrust, but nodded his agreement and escorted his wife from the room.

Ludo's heart began pounding again as he turned back to his fiancée. She swallowed hard and Ludo wondered if she might be sick.

"You must hate me," she said, staring at her feet.

Ludo hesitated, wondering what to say to her. Honesty seemed the best idea, yet he was afraid to say too much, to let her see how badly he wanted this.

"I don't hate you."

She looked up at him then, her lovely brown eyes filled with sorrow. "How can you say that? I have ruined your life. I imagine the last thing you ever wanted was a wife, let alone… let alone one like me."

That last bit was whispered, and she sounded so utterly defeated that his heart ached, but what on earth did she mean?

"One like you?" he repeated.

She got to her feet, her arms crossed around her waist.

"Don't make me spell it out," she said, irritated now, which was better than the awful sense that she'd been crushed, but he still did not understand.

"But I'm afraid I must, Miss Bunting. I do not know what you mean."

"Bunty," she corrected with an impatient huff before adding, "They call me Buxom Bunty, and that's the nicest of my nicknames, I assure you. Fat Felicity is another."

"Who said such a thing to you?" Ludo demanded, hearing the hurt in her voice and wanting to tear limb from limb whatever wretch had made her feel anything less than beautiful.

She gave him an odd look, as if he was being deliberately obtuse.

"Nigh on everybody," she retorted. "It's not as if it isn't true."

"The devil it is!"

Her eyes widened at his fierce response and he wondered why she looked so surprised by it. Had no one ever defended her?

"There is no need to be polite for the sake of it, my lord. In fact, I should vastly prefer it if there were complete honesty between us. I have no expectation that... that you should give up your...." He could see her struggle for a polite way of framing her words. "*Pursuits*. I have trapped you into this, though I swear I did not intend to do so. I do not expect you to... to woo me."

"Yet, I find that I would like to, all the same."

She gasped, staring up at him with obvious suspicion. "B-But why?"

Ludo dared to move closer to her, encouraged when she didn't take to her heels, but watched him come to her. To his chagrin, he realised his hand was shaking as he raised it to touch her cheek, the back of his fingers sliding against satin.

"So beautiful," he said, reverence in his voice.

Her mouth fell open in shock and he could not resist. He lent down and kissed her. She didn't move so much as a muscle and, when he pulled away, she was still staring at him. He wasn't certain if it was shock or horror in her eyes, and took a hasty step back.

"May I call on you again tomorrow?"

She nodded, silent, still staring at him.

Ludo looked around as her father returned to the room.

"Until tomorrow, then," he said, bowing to her, and leaving her alone.

***

8th December 1820. London.

Bunty sat by the window, watching the road. Then she got up and paced for a bit. Then she ran back to the window and stared at the road a bit more.

"Do stop acting like such a ninny," she scolded herself, yet there didn't seem to be any choice in the matter. Not since he had kissed her.

For the hundredth time since that extraordinary event, she raised her fingers to her lips, tracing the place his mouth had been. It had been such a gentle kiss: tender, and not what she had expected of such a man. Well, she had not expected to be kissed at all. She had expected fury, disgust, and recriminations at having been so ill used. If she were perfectly honest, she had not expected him to pursue her. She assumed he would have been relieved that she would not hold him to marrying her, and take to his heels. *It had to be the dowry*, said the sensible voice in her head, the one that would not let her get her hopes up. Her hopes had been crushed too many times for her to believe in them again, and yet….

He had said she was beautiful.

Why would he say such a thing to her? He had chosen to act the gentleman and marry her, and he would have her dowry. There was no need to woo her to secure her money. It would be his, to do with as he pleased, for Papa had warned her his finances were not what one would hope for. Not that she cared. If she could believe for a moment that he might like her, that he might even come to care for her, she would not pine for a fortune.

Who said such a thing to you?

The anger in his voice as he'd demanded who had insulted her had been a shock, too. It had been instantaneous, and she had believed it to be genuine. Yet it seemed so odd. Lord Courtenay was known to be seen in the company of all the most beautiful of the Cyprians. He might not have money, but he was so big, handsome, and obviously virile that even the exclusive highflyers sought him out. She could not make him out at all.

The sound of horses outside the door had her looking up, and there he was. He had sent a note earlier to inform her he would take her for a drive, and to wrap up warm. It was a bright, sunny winter's day, but still chilly, and Bunty had dressed in deep plum velvet carriage dress. Hoping she looked as well as she might, she snatched up her reticule and hurried to the front door.

"Miss Bunting," he said, giving her a formal bow. He paused, a slow smile curving over his mouth. "How lovely you look."

Bunty searched his face for any sign that he was mocking her, yet she found nothing but pleasure in his eyes. Heavens, she'd never seen eyes as blue as his before.

"Good day, my lord," she said, wishing she could still the erratic thumping of her heart.

She was being idiotic.

He offered her his arm and led her outside, where a smart yellow-and-black Phaeton awaited them. One of her father's footmen held the horses, two glossy bays who tossed their heads impatiently.

"How lovely," she said as he handed her up.

Lord Courtenay settled beside her, and Bunty felt a jolt of surprise as his strong thigh pressed against hers. He was a large man and took up a deal of space. So large, in fact, that for the first time in her life, Bunty did not feel as though the rest of the world had been made in miniature. In comparison, she could almost believe herself dainty.

He nodded to the groom who released the horses. They set off at a smart trot and Bunty dared a glance at him, only to see he was regarding her in turn.

"I'm afraid they're not mine," he said, and she was struck by how awkward he appeared. "The horses and... all of it."

He shrugged his massive shoulders and Bunty's mouth went dry.

"I expect your father told you I'm no catch," he added, and there was a defensive note in his voice which surprised her.

"And yet," she said, "I've no doubt there are women a-plenty who would cut off their right arm to be sitting where I am."

He snorted in disgust. "No one like you, Miss Bunting."

She frowned at him and he shook his head, looking vaguely bewildered.

"You still don't believe me, do you?" he said. "You think I'm bamming you, flattering you for no good reason."

It was Bunty's turn to shrug, and she looked away, unable to hold his piercing gaze.

"Why would I do that?" he asked. "I did not have to marry you, I chose to. If I only wanted your money... well, it will soon be mine. What reason could I have to say such things to you?"

It was everything she had told herself, and it sounded so reasonable as he echoed her thoughts. Bunty forced herself to look back at him.

"Then perhaps it is simply that you are kind, my lord. I have often believed it of you. You always smiled at me with such... warmth, but I cannot believe you are content with this arrangement."

Something dark flashed in his eyes and she knew she was right. Oh well, better to have the truth unvarnished than live a lie. She tried to make herself believe that, but her heart ached all the same.

"No. I was not happy to discover it was not me you intended for your trap, but Lord Stanthorpe. Not that I could blame you for that."

Was that *regret* in his voice?

"Tommy is the best of fellows. Kind and funny and good-natured. Rich, too, and an earl, to boot. I don't suppose that hurts," he added bitterly.

Bunty gaped at him. Was he… jealous? No. That was utterly ridiculous.

"But I didn't mean to trap Tommy," she said in a rush, her heart thudding even though she refused to believe what she was hearing.

He narrowed his eyes and her breath caught at being the object of his scrutiny. "Miss Bunting, you told me so yourself."

"No!" Bunty shook her head. "Oh, you've got it all wrong."

He was silent for a moment as he navigated a busy stretch of road, but then Hyde Park stretched before them, quiet now on a chill winter's day.

"Well then, Miss Bunting," he said, once he could return his attention to her. "I wish you would explain it to me."

"Please, call me Bunty. Everyone does."

He nodded but said nothing, and Bunty explained just what had happened last night. She told him of the Ratched sisters' plans, of how she had warned Tommy and then gone back to confront Sylvia.

He was silent throughout her explanation until he drew up in a copse of trees, a secluded spot ideal for an illicit rendezvous. Bunty shifted nervously in her seat.

"So, in fact, you were not in the market for a husband at all," he said, and she could not read his expression, nor his tone of voice.

She gave him the benefit of an exasperated look. "My lord, I am five and twenty. I have been in the market for a husband these last seven years and have simply failed to catch one. I was not, however, so desperate as to stoop to trickery and subterfuge."

He stared at her for a long moment, that blue gaze studying her so thoroughly she had to fight to hold it. At length, he sighed, and looked so dejected Bunty wanted to reach out and take his hand. She folded her own in her lap.

"So, you set no trap. You were acting honourably, saving a friend from disaster, and facing down his enemy for him. Tommy is lucky indeed to have you on his side. You are brave and bold, Miss Bunting."

Bunty blushed, unused to hearing herself described in such a light. "Nonsense. Anyone would have done the same."

He gave a little huff of amusement. "No. They would not, and that you could still believe that shows exactly the kind of person you are."

"A fool, you mean," she said tightly, quite used to her parents telling her she was too naïve, too willing to look for the good in people who would end up using her for their own ends.

"No!" he exclaimed, his dark brows pulling together. He shifted on the seat, turning towards her, which pressed his knee harder against hers. "Not that. Never a fool, Bunty."

Bunty stared at him, unable to work this strange creature out. What did he want from her, this beautiful man who looked like a god, who was supposed to be wicked and wild? He was meant to be the worst kind of rake, and yet had such kindness in his eyes, and he was looking at her now like… like….

"Bunty," he said, his voice low.

"Y-Yes?"

"I should like to kiss you."

"Oh."

Bunty's heart gave an odd little kick in her chest and she felt an awful blush creep up her chest, up her neck, heating her face. Good lord, she must be scarlet by now. How dreadfully unattractive and gauche. He grinned at her and reached out, touching her cheek.

"Such a pretty colour," he murmured. "I love that you blush so easily. I wish I could see where the colour begins."

"My lord!" she exclaimed, wondering why she wasn't cross with him for having said such a thing, but she was not. Shocked, yes, but not a bit cross.

"I'm sorry," he said, the sheepish look he gave her quite adorable, even though wickedness still glinted in his eyes. "I know I ought not say such things, but I've never been good at dissembling, at saying the right thing, the polite thing. I'm not polite at all, but I suppose you know that."

"Not in the least," Bunty replied, wishing she did not sound so breathless, but his fingers were still caressing her cheek. She had the urgent desire to lean into his touch, like a cat. Good heavens. "As I said, you were always kind. Unlike many of your ilk."

"In what way was I kind?"

His fingers trailed along the line of her jaw, down her neck, and Bunty shivered.

"You never ignored me. You smiled at me, and not in a mocking way, but like we might be friends if we were introduced. I appreciated that more than you'll know."

"Bunty," he said, and the way he said her name, all soft and low, made her breath catch in her throat. She looked up at him, struck by the way his eyes had darkened. "That wasn't kindness, love. I have so wanted someone to introduce us, but no one would let a devil like me near such a prize. The only way I could be near you was to fall into a trap set for another, but perhaps it was fate."

A prize? Bunty's mind had grown fuzzy at his proximity. He was leaning closer to her and his scent filled her mind. He smelled of clean linen, soap, and something male and musky that made her insides tremble with longing. She could hardly comprehend what he was saying. Her brain had fallen into a swoon when he'd said her name so softly, and it showed no signs of reviving.

"May I kiss you now?"

"K-Kiss?" she murmured hazily, blinking at him.

His mouth was so close to hers, his full lips sensuous, and the urge to press her mouth to his was overwhelming. So she did. His lips were soft and warm and... oh good heavens. She'd kissed him!

She drew back with a gasp, covering her mouth with her hand.

"*Oh!*" she said in horror. Good God, what would he think of her now? That she was a brazen hussy, most likely. Mortified, she lifted her gaze to find him looking down at her in amusement.

"Well, don't stop there," he said, one large hand moving to her waist. He leaned in again and nuzzled at her cheek, his voice a delicious whisper against her skin. "Do it again."

Bunty swallowed, wondering if she dared.

"*Please*," he added.

Well, how could she resist when he asked so nicely?

His mouth was so close she only had to move a little and their lips touched again. Bunty let out a shaky breath, overwhelmed by how sweet it felt to kiss him. She pressed a little firmer and withdrew and he only watched her, saying nothing, not moving.

Bunty kissed him again, a soft press of lips, followed by another, and another, and oh, it was lovely but... she wanted more.

"I don't know what I'm doing," she admitted.

"Are you sure?" he asked, and she was struck by how dark his eyes had grown, the black swamping the blue. His voice was low and breathless too, and he licked his lips, as though tasting hers.

Bunty's own breath hitched. "Sure about what?"

"That you don't know what you're doing. It seems to me that you are quite adept."

Bunty frowned, uncertain if he was sincere.

"Don't tease me," she said quietly. "I know there must be far more."

"I wasn't teasing, but yes... there's more."

"Show me, then."

No doubt she was an unattractive shade of puce by now, but there was nothing to be done about that. Besides, he'd said he liked her blush. Strange man.

"With pleasure."

Bunty gasped as he took her in his arms and held her close before his mouth covered hers. His kisses were nothing like hers had been. There was nothing shy or tentative about the way his mouth sought hers, or the way his tongue traced the seam of her mouth. *His tongue!* Bunty gasped and went to pull back, but he held her there, his tongue invading her mouth and stroking and... pleasure rolled through her. The day was cold, and their secluded spot out of the sun chillier still, yet Bunty was burning up. A slow fire had begun low in her belly and melted everything it touched until her bones were molten and everything beneath her flesh simmered. She was pliant in his arms, willing to go where he led, willing to do almost anything to keep the delicious liquid heat spilling through her body. His hand moved over her, up from her waist, moving slowly higher as Bunty's pounding heart reached a crescendo. She held her breath as he carried on higher still to cup her full breast. He caressed and gently squeezed, and even through all the layers of material the sensation was incredible. Bunty moaned with pleasure.

"Christ," he murmured, eyes wide as he broke the kiss.

Bunty was slammed back to reality in an instant.

Good God, what was wrong with her? She'd let him ravish her in the middle of Hyde Park, and would have allowed him a great many more liberties if he hadn't stopped. Where were all the lessons her mother had taught her? *Gone.* Burned away in the passion he had made her feel. No wonder he was considered so bloody dangerous.

"I'm so sorry," she said, wanting to die. "I don't know what c-came over me...."

"Sorry?" he repeated, obviously perplexed, and she thought perhaps a little annoyed too. "What the devil are you sorry for?"

Bunty hesitated. "N-Nice girls aren't supposed to behave like that."

He let out a sigh and reached for her, cupping her cheek. "You're the nicest girl I have ever met, and I loved every minute of it. Please don't regret it, but I suppose I had better take you home. We're not married yet."

"Why?"

Lord Courtenay frowned at her. "Why what?"

"Why are you marrying me?"

He hesitated and Bunty held her breath, for once in her life allowing herself to hope for a man to say something that did not make her feel unattractive and unwanted. He turned and looked at her, his expression intent.

"Not for your dowry, if that's what you're wondering. I'm not marrying you because I must, and I'm not marrying you for your money. I swear upon my honour, for whatever that tarnished article may be worth to you."

Bunty smiled at him. It wasn't exactly a romantic declaration, but it was more than she'd dared hope for. "I think your honour is a most valuable thing, my lord."

He stared at her, something in his eyes that she could not read.

"Thank you," he said softly. "And it's not 'my lord.' Not anymore. I should like you to call me Ludo."

Chapter 3

"Wherein Lord Courtenay takes a wife."

8th December 1820. London.

Ludo stared around his rented rooms, trying to see through the eyes of a gently raised young woman who had been bred for greater things than this blasted hovel.

Hell and damnation.

Oh God, what had he done? She would take one look at this dump and walk straight out again. He could take her to a hotel for their wedding night, but… but this would still await them the next day. She'd see then exactly what a pitiful excuse for a man she'd married. She hadn't realised yet, the poor girl. For the moment, his looks had charmed her, just as they'd charmed so many other women before her. They ought to be good for something, he thought bitterly, after having ruined his life in every other way. The Courtenay family were all fair-haired, with green or hazel eyes. His father and his two older brothers fitted the mould perfectly: medium height, medium build, sandy hair, fair skin and green eyes. And then there was Ludo. Standing well over six feet, he was built like an ox, with hair the colour of midnight, skin that spoke of Mediterranean climes, and eyes of bright blue.

A cuckoo in the nest if ever there was one.

In the days before she'd died, his mother had told him his father had been an Italian count. The handsomest man she had ever met. Her lover had wanted her to run away with him, but she had not wanted Ludo to live with the ensuing scandal. God, how he wished his mother *had* run, and taken him with her. It could not possibly have been worse.

Ludo reached down, picked up an empty brandy bottle and set it on the mantel. He was getting married tomorrow. This would not do. He needed help.

An hour later, he returned to his rooms with three of his favourite ladies from the brothel around the corner. They had not been best pleased at being woken during daylight hours, but the promise of being paid double their usual rate—and the lure of one of their favourite customers—had got them moving.

"Well then, lover," Jenny said, pressing herself against him with a suggestive smile. "What's got you all riled up, then? Three of us going to be enough, is it? He's in the mood for some sport, I reckon, girls."

The other two women giggled, and Ludo sighed, hoping they would not hate him for asking for their help.

"No sport, Jen. I'm sorry. The truth is, I'm getting married tomorrow."

They stared at him.

"Oh!" Sarah said, her face clearing. "He wants to sow the last of his wild oats."

"Bleedin' 'ell," Rachel crowed. "I don't reckon 'e's got none left!"

The three of them fell about laughing and Ludo sighed, unhooking Jenny's arms from his neck.

"No, no. You've got it all wrong. Please, ladies. I need your help. I'd not ask otherwise. I'm getting married and the poor girl is getting a wretched bargain as it is, without… without bringing her back to… to this…." He gestured about him in despair. "I know I'm a devil for asking it of you, but please? Help me make it look a bit less…."

"Like a tomcat's hideaway?" Jenny suggested, raising one eyebrow.

"Exactly," Ludo replied, relieved.

Jenny tutted at him and folded her arms. "Not sure we ought to help him, girls, not if it means he's going to be a proper husband and mend his ways."

Rachel snorted. "When did gettin' married ever stop a bloke from having his fun? Won't change nothin'."

Jenny studied Ludo for a long moment, and he felt a wave of heat burn up the back of his neck. "Nah. Ludo's a good 'un," she said softly. "If he says his vows, they'll mean summat. Won't they, love?"

Ludo nodded, something in his chest constricting at being read so easily, when he'd hardly dared acknowledge the truth himself.

"She a nice girl?" Jenny asked, smiling at him.

Ludo nodded. "Better than I deserve, Jen."

"Ah, come on then, ladies. Roll your sleeves up. Let's help the poor sod get his house in order."

"Do we get summat for our trouble when it's done, eh?" Sarah asked him, moving close enough to run her hand over his chest and down to more intimate areas.

Ludo caught hold of her wrist and raised her hand to his lips, kissing her fingers. "A generous purse and my undying gratitude, Sarah."

The girl heaved a sigh and rolled her eyes. "Ah, well. As you like, handsome."

By late afternoon, Ludo's rooms had been thoroughly cleaned and aired, fresh sheets put on the bed, and an embarrassing number of empty bottles disposed of. Once the girls had gone, each of them in possession of a generous sum for their troubles, Ludo had headed out to buy a wedding ring. A simple gold band was all he could afford, but his hopes rose exponentially on seeing the ring tucked into its little red box. A new beginning, he promised himself. On the way back, he'd noticed a flower seller, her basket crammed full of Christmas roses. He made the girl's day by buying the entire basketful. It would be an excellent way of brightening up his less than elegant abode and, besides which, the flowers made him think of Bunty.

Ludo stared down at the large bouquet in his hand and laughed as he walked home. This was his last night as a bachelor. No doubt he ought to be out drinking with his friends and making the most of his freedom. He couldn't think of anything he wanted to do less. He had caroused and debauched his way through life since he was a very young man, and now that was done. Now he would have a wife, someone to come home to, someone who gave a damn if *he* came home.

She *would* give a damn, wouldn't she?

Bunty was everything good in life. She was kind and brave and clever and... and she would give him a chance. He ran up the steps to the front door and let himself back into his rooms, feeling his heart sink to his boots as he realised no amount of cleaning and tidying would turn them into the kind of place Bunty would expect to live in—like a house in Mayfair.

Oh, God. She would hate him.

***

"Bunty, darling. I've been thinking. We were too hasty. You need not go through with it," her father said.

Bunty looked around from her sentry position by the front window to see her parents standing side by side.

"What?" she asked, a little irritated to have her attention taken from watching the road.

Lord Courtenay—Ludo — should be here soon. They were to be married at two o'clock. Her father had arranged the special licence and the minister was seated in the back parlour with a cup of tea whilst he awaited the arrival of her bridegroom.

"I did a little investigating about Lord Courtenay at my club yesterday, and the reports are far from good. Worse than we had realised, even. Your mother and I have been talking and… oh, Bunty. My dear child, we cannot help but think that in such circumstances, ruination might be better than marriage to… to such a man."

Bunty's eyes grew wide as she realised her father was in earnest.

"But, Father, I should be shunned by polite society. What would I do? Where would I go?"

"We thought perhaps your Great-Aunt Hildebrand," her mother said, her voice quavering. "She lives very quietly, no one there would know you, or would know about…."

She sobbed and buried her face in her handkerchief.

"You think I would be better served living with an old lady of eighty in the wilds of Cumbria than marrying Lord Courtenay?" Bunty replied, astonished and horrified.

"If it were any other man, my dear." Her father's eyes were filled with pity. "But Courtenay… Everyone knows he's a bastard, for all his father was duped into acknowledging him. He was disowned by his family, and he's raised hell at every opportunity since. He'll likely squander your fortune and subject you to heaven alone knows what indignities. He has no money, no prospects. What can you hope to gain by marrying him?"

"But it's all arranged," Bunty protested. "You went and got the licence; you agreed the terms with him. You cannot change your mind now."

"No," her father said, his voice firm. "But *you* can, and no one would think less of you for not marrying such a man."

Bunty stared at her father. She knew everything he'd said was likely true. It was impossible to deny the accusations against Ludo. The scandals were legion, his reputation blacker than pitch. *Leopards don't change their spots*, whispered a little voice in her head.

Her breath caught as she heard the front door close and, a moment later, the butler announced him. Bunty's heart thudded as Ludo appeared in the doorway. Oh, but he was magnificent. His powerful thighs were clad in buff breeches, the embroidered cream waistcoat and dark blue coat exquisitely cut, highlighting his impressive physique. Bunty could not draw a breath at all as he bowed low to them and then moved towards her, smiling with such warmth that she wanted to cry.

"Miss Bunting," he said, a look in his eyes that was just for her as he lifted her hand to his lips and kissed it. "How lovely you look. I am the most fortunate of men."

Tears stung her eyes as she realised he was sincere. He truly thought her lovely.

"My lord." Bunty jumped at the force of her father's voice. "We have spoken with our daughter, and there has been a change of plan. There is something she would like to say to you."

Ludo stiffened, looking from her father back to her. Bunty flushed, horrified and uncertain of what to say, until she saw the hurt in his eyes. It was only there for a moment before his expression was wiped clean. He stood tall and did not meet her gaze.

"Of course," he said, with no inflection in his voice. "I quite understand. There is no need to distress yourself, Miss Bunting. I believe I know what you wish to say."

He bowed, stiff and formal, and turned away from her.

Panic gripped Bunty at the terrible idea she might lose her chance to know this man better, to know more of the tender soul who had kissed her as if she was everything he'd ever wanted, who had told her she was lovely and actually meant it. She reached out and grasped his arm.

"Wait!"

He stilled utterly, but did not turn back to her.

"Is that it?" she said, hearing her voice trembling. "You've nothing to say, no argument to make?"

Slowly, he lifted his eyes to hers, and she was drowning in all that lovely blue.

"What can I say, Miss Bunting? I knew from the first it was too good to be true. It was just a lovely daydream. Nothing more."

He went to move away again, but she held on tighter.

"No. I do *not* release you from your promise. Either you marry me or… or I shall s-sue you for breach of promise."

"Bunty!" exclaimed her father in horror as her mother shrieked and collapsed back onto the sofa.

Bunty ignored them both, her eyes fixed on Lord Courtenay, but his expression was unreadable.

"I do not release you," she said again. "The minister is waiting for us."

He moved closer to her and took both of her hands in his, though he did not meet her eyes as he spoke, looking down at his feet instead, as if ashamed.

"Your parents are right to warn you off. Everything they say is true, no doubt."

"I know of your reputation," she said quietly. "I know of all the stories in the scandal sheets, but is that all there is to you? Is there not more?"

He did not answer, still avoiding her eyes, but Bunty pressed on.

"Will you be cruel to me, my lord? Will you gamble away my money and spend it on other women? Will you leave me alone and destitute when it is gone?"

"What? *No!*" he exclaimed, his blue eyes flashing. "God, no. I would never... *never*..." His voice cracked and he snapped his jaw shut and simply shook his head, his eyes still burning with anger.

Bunty smiled at him, knowing her instincts had guided her right. "I would like to get married now, Ludo. If... If you still wish to marry me, that is?"

"If I wish to?" he repeated, looking astonished, and then he let out a harsh breath. "I should like that above all things, Miss Bunting."

"Bunty," she corrected him gently.

"Bunty," he said, staring at her in such a way she blushed and looked away from him.

"Well," she said, trying not to sound as if she was trembling all over. "Let us not keep the minister waiting any longer."

***

Ludo was married. It was the most extraordinary thing. Any moment now he'd wake up. He waited on the front step for his wife to bid goodbye to her mama, who was weeping as if her only daughter was about to climb the steps at Tyburn. He could hardly blame the poor woman. If he ever had a daughter, and a bastard like him wanted to court her, he'd have the devil put on the first ship to New South Wales without a second thought. That he now had a wife, and might one day have a daughter too, hit him like a hammer blow. A family. He might have a family. Well, it was bound to happen, wasn't it? Sooner or later, and he would have to provide for them.

At least he'd cleared all his debts, he assured himself, as a hot, panicky sensation rose in his chest. It wasn't beyond the bounds of possibility that the business he'd begun would bring him a profit, too. His schoolmasters had not written him off, after all; they'd said he had a brain in his head. He'd done rather well, actually. Better than his brothers, not that it had done him the least bit of good. In fact, he thought his father—well, not *his* father, but his mother's husband—had hated him all the more for that.

At last the tearful farewells were done and Bunty joined him, taking his arm as he led her to the hired carriage. Ludo ignored her father's wrathful gaze as he guided the man's daughter down the stairs and handed her inside. One day, he promised himself, one day he would provide her with a carriage and four perfectly matched horses, she would have the finest clothes, a house on Mayfair, and whatever else she desired. He'd sell his soul to the devil himself if he must, but one way or another he would give her the life she deserved for being so brave, so bloody mad as to give herself into his keeping.

Ludo climbed in after his bride and closed the carriage door. All at once silence reigned as the carriage rocked into motion. He dared a glance at her to see her staring resolutely straight ahead. God, the poor thing must be terrified. He only hoped she wasn't already regretting her rash decision, for she'd not even seen where she would be living yet.

He gathered his courage and reached out to take her hand, relieved when she curled her fingers quite naturally about his.

"Lady Courtenay," he said, a little stunned to realise such a creature existed.

She laughed, a soft breathy sound that made his heart skip about in his chest like a newborn lamb.

"That will take some getting used to," she said.

"Why did you do it?" he asked, hardly daring to hear the answer.

Perhaps her father was a cruel tyrant who beat her, and he was her only means of escaping. It seemed the only rational explanation.

She bit her full lower lip, worrying at it and sending desire lancing through him like a lightning strike as he fought the need to kiss the reddened flesh better.

"The truth," he urged her, telling himself he had best know the worst now, before he had fallen any farther under her spell.

She looked up at him and he stared down into eyes of the softest brown, flecked with gold, bronze, copper. *Idiot.* He had no farther to fall. He was utterly spellbound.

"I believe in you," she said, and then laughed again, though he liked this sound rather less than before. "My parents think I am quite mad, but… but I told them I believed you were a good man, that you would try your best to be a good husband to me."

Ludo stared at her in awe. "You said that? Out *loud*?"

"Of course out loud," she said, giving him an odd look. "Else how would they have heard me?"

"They're right." He reached out and caressed her cheek. "You are quite mad."

She stiffened, and he hurried on before he made a mull of it all.

"But you were right, too, at least… I have not been a good man, Bunty, but I will do better. I have no idea how to be a husband either, but I shall try."

He winced, wondering how he had ever been considered an eloquent ladies' man. The skill seemed to have been lost to him the moment he found himself alone in the library with this astonishing woman. Had that really only been two days ago?

To his delight she reached up, covered the hand at her cheek with her own, and turned into it, kissing his gloved palm and then blushing furiously. He wanted badly to pull her into his arms and kiss her, here and now, but he did not dare. The likelihood of getting carried away was too strong, and he would not embarrass her for the world. So, he did nothing more than hold her hand for the rest of the journey until they arrived outside of his front door.

The humiliation of guiding her into his bachelor accommodation was worse than he'd expected, and his expectations had been pretty bloody low. His stomach clenched to see her in such a place. It was like taking a flawless diamond and throwing it down in the dirt. So when she turned and smiled at him with delight in her eyes, he was quite lost for words.

"You bought flowers," she said, moving to where he'd arranged them in whatever jugs and empty glasses he could find, and set them around the room. She touched her gloved finger to the white petals, and Ludo ached for her to touch him with such obvious pleasure.

"They're Christmas roses," he said. "They reminded me of you."

She looked up at once, staring at him.

"They did?" she asked, obviously sceptical. "Why?"

He shrugged, feeling strangely self-conscious. He'd flattered and seduced women enough in his day, but he'd never given his heart with the words before. It was surprisingly daunting, making him feel vulnerable and exposed. "They're perfect. They look beautiful and delicate, innocent, but they are strong and brave enough to bloom in the harshest of winters."

Her mouth formed a little 'o' of surprise and she blinked, her eyes glittering brightly.

"That… That is the nicest thing anyone has ever said to me," she whispered.

"It's the truth."

She stared at him a moment longer before returning her attention to the room. Her gaze fell upon two framed watercolours, and Ludo felt anxiety prickle down his back.

"Oh, these are lovely. So cleverly painted. Where did you get them?"

"Um...."

She turned to look at him. "Do you know the artist?"

"Y-Yes," he hedged.

"They're marvellous. Look at the candlelight burning indoors, shining through the windows of that beautiful house, and the way the twilight is making the skies all dim and yet glowing outside. You can almost feel the chill of autumn in the air and you know the fire inside is warm and cosy. It looks just the sort of place one would wish to live, as if nothing bad could ever happen there."

Ludo allowed that comment to unfurl inside him with a burst of pleasure, but said nothing, uncertain of how she would feel about his love of painting. It was suited to young ladies and maiden aunts, but was not a manly pursuit. That point had been hammered home early on, his family having made their feeling about his ambitions to be an artist abundantly clear.

"And you have a meal ready for us, too."

Ludo watched as she uncovered the dishes and inspected the cold supper he'd had provided by his landlady.

"It looks splendid," she said, smiling at him as she removed her bonnet and gloves.

"Are you hungry now?" he asked, wondering why he was asking such stupid questions when all he wanted was to take her to bed.

To his great relief, she shook her head, then set the hat and gloves aside and unbuttoned her pelisse.

"I'm too nervous to eat. And I don't say that very often," she admitted, with a self-deprecating laugh that sounded a touch brittle. She laid her coat on a chair and clutched her arms about her stomach, blushing before looking away from him.

She was nervous, he realised. Well, of course she was. This was her wedding night, and… Holy God, she was a virgin. Not that he hadn't known that. Of course he'd *known* that, but… but he hadn't really considered that… that she'd never… that no one had ever….

He'd be the first.

Damn that, he'd be her *only*.

Oh, Lord, what if he hurt her?

What if she *cried*?

Panic gripped him.

"Perhaps some champagne, then?" he suggested, darting from the room the moment she nodded. Ludo hurried through the bedroom and flung open the window to retrieve the champagne bottle he'd left there to chill. He slammed the window shut again before the room grew cold, but a merry fire blazed in the hearth and it was warm and welcoming. He eyed the bed with misgiving.

Don't be a bloody fool, he cursed. *Anyone would think* you *were a bloody virgin.*

Idiotically, he wished that he was. He wished he could redo the past and make it so he wasn't the man he'd become, but then he'd never have met her. *Stop it*, he scolded himself, clutching at the cork of the champagne bottle. *Have a drink and calm down, for the love of God.*

"What a cosy room."

Ludo leapt from his skin as he heard Bunty enter the room, and the cork flew from the bottle with a resounding *pop*.

Champagne gushed from the neck and Bunty gave a laugh and snatched up the glasses he'd left on the dresser, placing first one then the other beneath the torrent. Well, he hoped that was the last of the humiliations in store for him this evening and not an omen.

If not, he'd best just throw himself from the window and have done with it.

"And you call yourself a rake," he muttered crossly.

"Pardon?"

"Would you like some cake?" he said in a rush, improvising wildly and hoping to God there was some.

"No, thank you, this is splendid," she said, raising the glass.

Ludo watched, fascinated, as she licked her lips, and everything south of his navel grew taut.

Oh, God.

Please let him get through this night without making her cry or shaming himself.

He only prayed that some forgiving deity was listening with a kindly ear and did not seek to make an example of him. Well, in that case... it looked like he was on his own.

Chapter 4

"Wherein… a wedding night."

9th December 1820. London.

Bunty looked up to find Ludo watching her intently. Their eyes met and he cleared his throat, turning away and going to the fireplace to stoke the fire which was burning merrily and did not appear to need his attention. She frowned. If she didn't know better, she would have said he was nervous.

Pffft. Nervous?

Lustful Ludo the Libertine?

Hardly.

Yet she did not know how else to account for his behaviour. Unless, of course, he didn't desire her? The thought made her stomach clench. *Oh.* She'd just assumed, after the way he'd kissed her, that… but perhaps bedding someone was another thing entirely. Or perhaps he'd gone off the idea, or….

"What's wrong?"

Bunty jolted, a little alarmed to discover he was standing so close to her.

"N-Nothing," she stammered, and then changed her mind. If this marriage was going to have the slightest chance of succeeding, they must be honest with each other. "Well, actually, there is something…."

His face fell and he looked so utterly dejected she wished she'd kept her blasted mouth shut.

"I know it's awful," he said, one large hand raking through his hair and making it stick up all over the place. "I tried my best to make it presentable, but no amount of flowers and champagne will ever turn this hovel into a palace, I'm afraid."

"What?" She stared at him for a moment before she realised what he was talking about. "Oh, no, it's not that. Your rooms are charming."

He snorted with disgust.

"For a bachelor, certainly." He moved closer and took her by the shoulders. "I will do better for you, Bunty. I swear I will."

"Please don't worry. After all, there is my dowry now, and—"

Ludo shook his head, his mouth set in a firm line. "No."

"No?" She frowned at him, puzzled by the resistance in his voice.

"I'll… I'll find a way myself. That money is yours, to use as you see fit."

Bunty gaped, bewildered. "But I don't need a sum like that! Though, that you would give me access to it is… is more than I expected. Thank you, Ludo."

"Christ, you would thank me? For forcing you to live in this…." He gestured around him with a muttered curse and turned his back on her. "I suppose I ought to use your money to buy us somewhere decent to live, for your sake at least, but… but I want to do it by myself. God, I'm a selfish bastard."

Bunty smiled, understanding his dilemma. A man's pride was a fragile thing. Her mother had taught her that much.

"I am perfectly content to live here while you get things in order, Ludo. It is no hardship, I assure you."

Bunty had come from a well-run, elegant house, and she had never lacked any comfort, but she did not think life in these rather shabby rooms was enough to daunt her. Not if Ludo genuinely wanted her with him, but that brought her back to her original point.

"You are too kind," he said.

She could not decipher his tone so she moved closer so she could see his face.

"Ludo?"

He turned towards her, and Bunty gathered her courage.

"D-Don't... don't you want me?"

She watched him blink, such an incredulous expression on his face she might have laughed if she'd not been so anxious.

"What?"

"Oh," she said, twisting her hands together. "Don't make me say it again. It's only... I thought before that... that you did, and you said I was lovely, and I... well, I believed you, which was probably foolish of me, but... but if you meant it, why... w-why haven't you kissed me yet?"

"God," he said with feeling. "I'm a stupid bastard as well as a selfish one. What a catch you are, Ludo."

Bunty's eyes grew wide at his language, but she said nothing as he was moving closer, putting his arms around her, pulling her close.

"Not want you?" he said on a breath of laughter. "How could you think such a thing?"

"Well." Bunty licked her lips, trying and failing not to stare at his mouth. "You seemed so nervous, and I thought perhaps you didn't want to, or that you'd changed your mind."

Ludo groaned and pressed his forehead gently against hers.

"Forgive me. I'm such a fool, it's only...."

"Only?" she pressed as he paused, looking embarrassed.

"It's only I wanted everything to be perfect, but I have to bring you here to this wretched place and you must surely regret agreeing to marry me, and then I realised that you'd never… that you hadn't…. That you were a virgin, and I'm worried because I don't want to hurt you, and…." He huffed out a bitter laugh. "You'd think the one thing I could do with no trouble was take you to bed, but no, I'm a bundle of nerves and I can't even get that right."

"Oh." Bunty reached up and cupped his beautiful face, joy bubbling through her blood like the champagne bottle had burst inside her veins. "You wanted to make me happy."

He nodded.

"Ludo?"

"Yes," he said cautiously.

"I'm so very glad I married you."

"You are?"

Bunty nodded. "I think I made a wise choice, and I believe that everyone will see that one day, but I don't care how long it takes, as long as you are glad too?"

"Bunty," he whispered. "Oh, God, love. I've never been gladder of anything in my whole life."

She laughed then. "How foolish we both are. From now on we must speak our minds and not fret about what each other is thinking, but ask. Don't you agree?"

A slightly wicked glint lit his eyes, but he nodded.

"I do," he said. "Why don't you do that, then?"

"Do what?"

"Ask me what I'm thinking."

Bunty swallowed, a little daunted now, but determined not to be silly. "W-What are you thinking, Ludo?"

He leaned in and nipped at her earlobe, making her gasp, and then whispered in her ear. "I'm thinking I should like you to take your clothes off now."

Bunty blushed as an odd mixture of anxiety and excitement coiled low in her belly.

"Oh."

"Mmmm," he murmured, kissing a path down her neck before returning to nuzzle the tender spot beneath her ear. "I want to unwrap my prize."

"I thought you were nervous."

"I'm putting up a heroic fight."

"Oh. Well, go on, then," she said, aware that she was breathless but impressed she'd got the words out at all.

He took a step back and grinned at her before turning her around. She felt the brush of his fingers against the nape of her neck as he worked each fastening in turn and shivered. What clever fingers he had. He was far quicker than her maid, she thought, as her dress slithered to the ground. Bunty closed her eyes and wished she were slender. If only she'd known she was to marry such a man, she could have at least tried to lose weight, not that it had ever worked before. Oh well, it was too late now. She only hoped he wasn't expecting too much. With a gasp, she realised he had worked even faster than she'd anticipated. She was clad only in her stockings and chemise, and Ludo was turning her back to face him. Panic struck her. She clutched her arms about her middle, wanting to hide as much of herself as possible. He would not allow that, though. He undid the tie of the chemise and gently moved her arms aside, before pushing the flimsy material down to join the rest of her clothes.

Bunty squeezed her eyes closed with mortification and prayed he was not disappointed.

***

Holy God and all his angels

Ludo let out a ragged breath as he stared at his wife in wonder. *You lucky bastard, Ludo.* He had no idea what the devil he'd done to earn this astonishing gift, surely nothing in this lifetime, but he swore he'd do whatever it took to be worthy of it.

He could hardly breathe. He longed to touch her but felt he ought not, as if it wasn't his right, yet he was her husband. She was his wife. *His wife!* He blinked hard as a sudden surge of emotion caught him off guard.

"Ludo?"

He looked up, to discover Bunty peering at him from between her fingers.

"Yes, love?"

"I'm trying hard not to jump to the conclusion that you don't want to touch me, b-but what is taking so long?"

Ludo let out a bark of laughter and then forced his expression into something more solemn as she glared at him in outrage.

"Forgive me," he said, his voice low and gravelly as desire thrummed through him. "I was so overwhelmed by my own good fortune, I could do nothing but stare. My God, Bunty, how lovely you are. I cannot help but fear I shall wake up in the morning and discover the whole thing has been a dream."

She gave him a sceptical glance and wrapped her arms about herself again, a gesture he was recognising as a habit, and thoroughly disliked. He moved closer and took each wrist in turn, moving her arms aside, allowing him to stare down at a delicious landscape of full breasts and luscious curves. His mouth watered.

"Don't you dare try to hide from me, wife." He released her wrists in favour of cupping her breasts and groaned as the plump weight filled his hands, heavy and ripe. "I do not understand how such a thing is possible, when everyone was so certain I'd go to the fiery pits, but I've died and gone to heaven."

"Don't be silly," she said, laughing, though it was a nervous sound.

Ludo looked at her curiously. "You have no idea, do you? You don't have the faintest idea what the sight of you does to me?"

She shook her head and Ludo smiled. "That's all right, love. I'll show you, but I tell you now, I've seen nothing as lovely as you in my whole life."

That he'd seen more than his fair share was something he didn't mention. He did not doubt that she knew it.

Ludo kissed her then, delighted at her eager response, that she remembered everything he'd taught her as she opened her mouth, her tongue seeking his. He kissed her until she was breathless and trembling, unable to still his wandering hands from exploring the silky skin exposed for his pleasure. Working his way down her body, he kissed her neck and shoulder, working lower with as much patience as he could muster until his hands and mouth found her breasts. He sighed happily.

She gave a little squeak of surprise as his mouth closed over her, suckling at her breast with enthusiasm before moving to the other and lavishing the same attention there.

"Oh," she said, a wondering sound as her hands rested tentatively upon his hair.

"So sweet, Bunty," he murmured against her skin. "I just know you'll be even sweeter elsewhere."

He got to his knees, pressing kisses over the soft swell of her belly and hips, moving lower as her eyes widened and her breathing grew fast. She gasped and squealed as he wriggled his tongue into her belly button and then laughed and he sat back on his heels to grin at her.

"I love to hear you laugh."

"Really?" she asked doubtfully. "Is it *appropriate* at such a moment? I always thought… well… this was supposed to be serious, solemn."

Ludo pressed a kiss to her belly.

"Sometimes, yes," he said, savouring the feel of her skin against his cheek. "But there ought to be playfulness, too: fun, and pleasure above all things."

He held her gaze and moved lower, kissing the sensitive skin at the apex of her thighs. Her breathing hitched as he moved again, nuzzling the silky curls before parting the delicate folds that hid the little pearl of flesh he sought. With a sigh of pleasure he kissed her there, before teasing his tongue between the folds. She gasped and clutched at his hair.

"Oh! Oh, my."

Ludo chuckled and settled to his work, licking and teasing until she was squirming, and he was forced to hold her still.

"Oh, it was all true," she murmured, though now she held him in place, her beautiful skin flushed with pleasure. "You are a bad, bad man. Dreadful. Utterly wicked…."

"Yes, love, and all yours now," he murmured before looking up at her, dazed with his good fortune.

"All mine?" she repeated, as if she had doubted it.

Ludo frowned and got to his feet. "I meant what I said, love. Forsaking all others."

A slow smile curved over her mouth and she flung herself at him, holding him tightly. Ludo savoured the moment, happy and a little bewildered that she had not expected at least that much from him. What a bad bargain she had been willing to strike. He could not comprehend why she would take such a chance, for she was not so foolish as to be dazzled by a pretty face alone. Well, whatever her reasons, he would do his best, in all things, which reminded him….

He reached down and swept her up, laughing at the incredulity in her eyes as he lifted her with ease.

"Goodness, you're strong."

Ludo snorted. "You're a featherweight, love."

She made an incredulous sound. "Oh, what a plumper. I certainly am not anything of the sort."

He tsked with impatience and set her down carefully on the bed, leaning over her. "I don't know what kind of maggoty ideas you have in that head of yours. Though I suppose I ought to expect such nonsense from someone hen-witted enough to marry me, of all people, but let us dispense with this nonsense once and for all."

"What nonsense?" she said, eyeing him dubiously as he made his voice stern.

"The idiotic notion you have about being too heavy, too big, too fat, or whatever preposterous ideas you have about yourself."

Her dark brows drew together, and she shook her head. "I know you're being kind, Ludo."

"Damnation!" he said, throwing his hands up. "I'm not being kind, you little widgeon. I mean… just look at you…." He did just that, his breath catching as his gaze travelled over her body, laid out for him on his bed, *their* bed. "You're splendid, gorgeous, a bloody goddess, and I'm going to prove it to you."

***

Bunty stared up at him, astonished by the obvious desire in his eyes. He really meant it. He did not think her too tall, too plump, too… *everything*. Though she had never done so before, Bunty questioned why she thought she was. Well, because she'd been told so. Her mother was always imploring her to lose weight and father always looked disapproving if she ate a dessert. She'd been teased as a girl by those who were supposed to be her friends and she'd heard too many disparaging comments from men not to take them to heart, and yet….

And yet Ludo, this big, glorious man, was looking at her as if she were the last cake in the world, and he was starving.

It was rather… invigorating.

He'd said she was splendid, gorgeous, *a bloody goddess!*

For the first time in her life, Bunty rather thought she felt like one too.

He'd also said he would prove it to her. She wondered just how he intended to do that, but then she realised he was taking off his clothes, and thought of any kind was suspended.

He made rather a performance of it for her, sliding off his cravat and tossing it to her with a wink, before easing out of his coat. Slowly, he unbuttoned his waistcoat, his eyes never leaving hers, that heated and intense gaze making her insides quiver with anticipation. Once he cast it aside, he tugged the shirt from his breeches before pulling it over his head in one smooth movement.

Bunty's mouth went dry.

If she was splendid, he was… *magnificent.*

Big and broad, his shoulders and arms were impressive enough, and now she saw how he'd lifted her as though she'd been made of spun sugar. His chest, though…. Words failed her, though her fingers itched to touch him, to run her fingers through the fleece of coarse hair on his chest and touch the thick quilting of muscle beneath. The desire to rub herself against him like a cat was almost overwhelming, but then she realised he'd discarded his boots and stockings during her reverie, and his fingers had moved to unbutton the fall of his breeches. Bunty was riveted to the spot, filled with curiosity. She had seen the naked male form before, in sculpture at any rate. Not every figure had a strategically placed fig leaf, though she had always been a little underwhelmed by what she'd seen and wondered how that appendage had done the job required of it. All such questions were firmly—and appropriately—put to bed as Ludo pushed his breeches and small clothes to the floor, and kicked them to one side.

"Goodness," she squeaked.

Ludo smirked at her, and she covered her mouth with her hand as a giggle escaped.

He tilted his head to one side, narrowing his eyes.

"Are you laughing at me?" he demanded with mock outrage.

"N-No."

"You're a terrible liar."

"Oh, I'm s-sorry," she managed, struggling not to laugh. "Only you looked so d-dreadfully pleased with yourself."

"And why not?" he demanded, his dark eyebrows flying up. "You were looking at me in a way that made me feel about ten feet tall."

Bunty sighed as he moved closer. "You are rather splendid, Ludo. So handsome. Are you really mine?"

"Yes," he said firmly. "And there's no changing your mind now, it's too late. You're stuck with me."

Ludo climbed onto the bed and lay down beside her, his head braced on his arm, his eyes warm and mischievous. He looked happy, and Bunty could not help but smile in return.

"Good afternoon, Lady Courtenay."

"Good afternoon, my lord," she replied politely, for all the world as if they had just greeted each other in the park.

"May I debauch you now, my lady?"

Bunty choked out a laugh, only to see him grinning at her with such a boyish gleam of amusement that she threw back her head and laughed again.

"You're dreadful!" she exclaimed, and then caught her breath as he climbed over her. He stared down at her, his blue eyes bright and glinting with desire.

"Yes, and you like it, so you must be every bit as wicked. Let's find out, shall we?"

Bunty was only too happy to do so, sighing as he started where he'd left off. He kissed her everywhere, touching her reverently, caressing and painting intricate patterns with his tongue. The most shocking sounds were drawn from her until she was panting and clutching at the bedclothes, her skin damp as he returned to the sinful place between her legs and made her believe she might go mad as her body spun out of control. It was as though she had been an instrument, put away and forgotten, dusty and unused, and suddenly he had come to teach her how to play, for he seemed to know her body far more intimately than she had known it herself.

She wasn't even shocked when he slid a finger inside her; she only moaned her pleasure and revelled in the way he praised her for her lascivious behaviour. The louder she was, the better he seemed to like it.

"Say my name," he begged her, his voice husky as he slid another finger inside her and caressed until she saw stars. "I want you to come with my name on your lips."

She did not entirely understand what he was asking her for, but then he applied his mouth once more. Pleasure rolled over her, making her hold her breath as the onslaught became overwhelming. She clutched at his hair, at the bed, at anything that might keep her tethered to the earth for surely she would fly away.

"Ludo!" she cried, her body arching, his name torn from her as waves of incandescent joy surged through her, over and over until she was sated, boneless, and utterly spent.

She was only dimly aware of him kissing his way back up her body, and she blinked hazily at him as he settled between her legs. It was only as he slid that wicked, masculine part of him against her oversensitive flesh that she gasped, and her eyes flew open.

"Now?" she said, a little stunned.

"Definitely now," he agreed, sounding strained and determined. "Unless...?"

He hesitated, and Bunty laughed at the disappointment in his eyes.

"Now," she agreed, wrapping her arms about his neck.

"Thank God," he murmured, sliding his arousal against her in a slick glide that made her close her eyes, her head thrown back.

Bunty moved her hands over his shoulders, glorying in the shift and play of powerful muscle and the damp silk of his skin. The coarse hair on his torso felt delicious against her breasts as he pressed closer, reaching between them to guide himself inside her.

"Speak to me."

Bunty blinked up at him in bewilderment. He wanted conversation? *Now?*

"Tell me it's all right. I don't want to hurt you."

Oh.

"Bunty?"

"It's all right. Don't stop, it's...." She sucked in a breath as she reconsidered that statement and he stilled utterly. For a moment, she breathed carefully around the strange sensation, and then she relaxed by degrees.

"Better?" he asked, his voice strained.

She could feel the tension singing through him.

"Yes."

He moved again, cautiously, slowly, and Bunty stared up at him. He had his eyes closed, his face a picture of concentration. How beautiful he was, and how careful of her. He was tender and thoughtful and... and how had this man gained such a reputation? How had he become what he was purported to be? She could see nothing of that in him now. His eyes flicked open, dazzling blue and filled with triumph as he gazed down at her. Bunty smiled.

"Better?" he asked again, his lips quirking.

"Better," she agreed, and then gasped as he tilted her hips and... *oh.*

"Much better," he said this time, and it wasn't a question. He sounded rather smug.

"Oh, yes... m-much...."

Bunty wrapped herself about him and simply held on, clinging to his powerful frame as he taught her what pleasure was, what they could have together. And, oh, it was marvellous. His touch was careful, his attention on her absolute. At this moment, she hadn't the slightest doubt she was the centre of his universe, and she wanted to be there always. The intimacy was astonishing, the closeness with this man she barely knew. Already, she felt he had sunk into her bones, into her soul. She *did* know him, didn't she? At least she recognised his generosity, his kindness, and his willingness to share himself—both his faults and his strengths— and to bolster her own insecurities with his surety. Bunty was lost, drowning in him, in this man she had known so little but was falling for like a star plummeting to earth. His body made hers sing, made her feel right in her own skin in a way she'd never thought possible. No longer was she awkward and hiding herself, trying to disguise her curves, to diminish her height. He loved her body, that much was obvious from the way he was moving, every grunt of pleasure that made her skin prickle with awareness. She had never realised, never expected.... Her mother's staccato, anxiety-laden words of advice for her wedding night had not given the slightest hint that this... *this* was even possible. Perhaps it wouldn't be with anyone else but him, but it *was* him. He was breathing hard now, his movements erratic and harsh, wonderfully masculine sounds of effort and passion filling her ears as he shuddered, jerked, and spilled himself inside her with a hoarse cry that made her heart soar, and hope fill her to the brim.

He collapsed on top of her with a groan, his chest heaving, his body slick with the effort of his exertions. Bunty lay pinned beneath him, feeling a little dazed and very feminine and... and almost delicate as his heavy body pressed her into the mattress. It was heavenly.

"Christ, I'm crushing you," he muttered, hauling himself up.

"No!" Bunty cried, holding onto him and pulling him back. "No. Don't... Don't go. Not yet. I... I like it. I like the weight of you, the feel of you."

He shifted a little, propping his head on his elbow and staring down at her.

"You do, eh?"

There was teasing in his expression, but it was warm and gentle, in no way mocking, and so she just nodded.

"You've really gone and done it now, my lady," he said, his voice softer now. "You're mine."

"Yes."

"No regrets?"

Something flickered in his eyes, something vulnerable and uncertain, and Bunty wanted to chase it away. She reached her hand up to stroke his face, still unable to believe this gorgeous man was really hers.

"Not one," she said.

Chapter 5

"Wherein the real world intrudes."

13th December 1820. London.

"There's no choice, Ludo. If you will be so ridiculously stubborn about using my money, then we must not waste yours. Your landlady charges a fortune for those meals she cooks. We must either go out to eat, or get some shopping so I may attempt to cook for us, though I warn you now I am more than a little doubtful as to my skills."

"I won't have you skivvying and cooking!"

Bunty rolled her eyes as their discussion went around in a complete circle for the second time. "Then employ a maid and let us get some dinner."

Ludo was sitting up in bed, looking mutinous. His arms were folded across his chest and Bunty tried not to get distracted by the way it made his muscles bulge. She wanted to lick him. He was so delicious, and….

No.

Then he'd have his way, and they could not carry on like this. No matter how delightful it was.

They had not left his rooms in the five days since they'd married. Astonishingly, no one had called. Astonishing that was, until she realised her father had not posted notice of their marriage. He was ashamed of it. Of them. The knowledge burned, especially when she was so happy, but… well, that was her parents' problem. They only knew Ludo by reputation. They would come around when they realised the man he really was. The one she was coming to know.

"But I don't want to go out," he grumbled. "Come back to bed."

He gave the mattress an inviting pat.

Bunty wavered before firming her resolve. "*No.* And it's only for a while. Honestly, anyone would think you were ashamed of...."

She let those word hang in the air as she actually thought about them, and all her old insecurities came crashing down on her.

"Oh, no!" he said, and she looked up, startled by his impatient tone.

He leapt out of bed and crossed the room. She had been standing by the window in her dressing gown, staring at the street below. Now she was riveted to the sight of her husband striding towards her in all his naked glory. Her breath caught and held as he closed the distance between them and took her face in his hands, staring down at her.

"What maggoty idea has taken hold in that brain of yours, wife? For, if you think I could ever be ashamed of you... My God, that's a laugh. I've never been prouder of anything in my entire life, and that's a fact."

Bunty's gasped, a knot of emotion in her throat.

"Really, Ludo?" she asked, believing him but wanting to hear it again.

She had never known what it was to be so thoroughly approved of, to be with someone—*anyone,* let alone a man—who looked at her as though she was important, as if *her* opinion mattered. Yet it was better even than that, for Ludo looked at her as if she was the beginning and the end of his world. She had tentatively begun to believe he meant it.

"Of course, really," he said, impatient now, and then his expression darkened, and his voice was filled with regret, "it's you who will be ashamed, love."

Bunty took a moment to look him over, feeling a now familiar surge of heat as desire pooled in her belly. She shook her head and smiled at him.

"Now who's having maggoty ideas?"

He gave a huff of laughter, but it was bitter-edged, and she did not like the sound of it. He turned away from her.

"If we go outside that door, you will realise this is all I'm good for."

Bunty watched as he waved a dismissive hand at the bed.

"Don't be foolish, Ludo," she said, thinking perhaps he was joking, but the way he was dragging on his small clothes and then his breeches with sharp, angry movements made her reconsider.

"Fine," he muttered "You want to go out? We'll go out. You'll figure it out eventually, anyway."

"Ludo," she protested, wondering where this unhappy, angry man had come from when he'd been so content just moments earlier.

She ought not have pressed him, ought not have insisted but… but no, this was silly. They were only going out to eat. It wasn't Almack's, not that they'd have a hope of gaining entry there, she thought with amusement and a complete absence of regret. Goodness, she could just imagine the patronesses' elegant noses turn up in horror if she turned up with….

Oh.

"Ludo."

He did not answer, searching for a clean shirt before giving up and snatching the one he'd married her in off the floor. He'd not worn one since.

"Ludo," she said again, as he tugged the shirt over his head.

She moved to him, standing right before him and clutching at the billowing fabric so he had to give her his attention. He stilled, his eyes wary, tension rolling off him in waves.

"What?" he asked, terse and irritated, but not, she thought, with her.

"Ludo, you know how you don't understand how I have always felt so… so uncomfortable with… with the way I look?"

Ludo rolled his eyes and muttered something under his breath, and Bunty smiled.

"Precisely," she said, sliding her hands about his waist. "You do not understand it because, by some happy miracle, you do not see me like everyone else does."

"Nonsense," he snapped. "It's only that you've let your mother dress you and hidden yourself away in corners, trying to make yourself shorter and skinnier, and something you're not. You're beautiful, inside and out, and everyone else would see it too, if you'd only believe it yourself."

Bunty blinked away the emotion those words produced and reminded herself that she was reassuring him this time. It was only fair, after all, not to mention God's honest truth.

"Well, perhaps," she allowed, her voice quavering. "But the point is, Ludo, you're wrong about what I think, about how I shall feel outside of these doors. I know your reputation. I followed your exploits, you know. I always searched the scandal sheets for your name to see what you'd been up to. I expect I know more about you than you do yourself, though I suspect much of it was fabrication, or at least the truth with fancy embroidery. I know all those things, and now I am coming to know *you*, and I'm proud of you. I'm proud of you, and not only because you're so handsome you make my heart feel all strange and fluttery, but because you're wonderful. You're kind and funny and generous…. Oh, Ludo, don't let other people's opinions spoil everything, for I shan't."

She watched his throat work, saw the doubtful glint in his eyes and pressed on, determined to get her point across.

"You made me believe in myself, Ludo. You've made me feel beautiful these past days, and I shall continue to believe it no matter what others say, so long as you always think it. So believe in my words too... *please?*"

He pulled her into his arms and held her close, resting his head atop hers. He said nothing for the longest time and then looked down at her, one dark eyebrow quirking. "Strange and fluttery?"

Bunty laughed. "Oh, Ludo, that's the bit of my heartfelt declaration that stuck in your head, was it?"

He gave her an odd look. "I'm a man, of course it was."

She huffed and shook her head, giving in. "Yes, my beautiful man. Looking at you, thinking of you... it does peculiar things to my heart."

"Not just your heart," he said, waggling his eyebrows at her.

Bunty spluttered and buried her face in his shirt.

"Dreadful," she said despairingly.

Ludo touched her chin with his fingers, raising her face to his and bending down, kissing her with such tenderness that tears pricked at her eyes.

"You make me believe I could be something," he said quietly. "And I want to be, for you. I want that very badly."

Bunty swallowed and gave a decisive nod. "You already are, Ludo, but I believe you can be anything you want. I believe in you."

***

Ludo took Bunty to Abingdon's chop shop and watched his wife with the greatest of pleasure as she took in her surroundings. That she had never been to such a place in her life was evident, as her fascinated gaze swept over everything and everyone. At first he'd hesitated, uncertain he should take her inside, but… well, they had to eat, and she was right. If he was dead set against spending her money—which he knew was idiotic, but had stuck in his brain as a matter of principle—then it was either this or making her cook for them, and that he would not do. She had been raised a lady, raised with the expectation and ability to run a large and prosperous household. A woman who might have married an earl, or at least a viscount, not some disowned, disgraced youngest son with nothing but his tarnished name to claim as his own.

As he'd opened the door, he'd wished he was taking her somewhere fancy, that he could afford Claridge's or Grillon's, but now, watching her, he rather thought she preferred this. It was a bustling place with the rich scent of roasted meat heavy on the air. Ludo's stomach growled as he realised how hungry he was. A harried waiter came up and took their orders, slapped a jug of ale on the table, and gave the scarred top a perfunctory wipe with a grubby cloth before hurrying away again.

Ludo poured them each a glass and watched with amusement as Bunty took a cautious sniff and then sipped. She screwed up her face and shuddered, then resolutely took another sip. By the fifth sip she seemed to have the hang of it, and Ludo reached his hand across the table, an odd sensation in his chest as he stared at her. She had always been a far-off dream, a bright hope he'd never dared want, for it was too implausible, too fantastic that she would ever look at someone like him, but here she was. His wife. Emotion filled his heart, pushed at his ribs, something new and fragile and optimistic, and he dared to let it flare to life instead of snuffing it out as he had with every other thing he'd ever wanted for himself. His hand was on the table, palm up. He felt silly, vulnerable, and went to withdraw it, except she noticed then that he had reached for her, and put her hand in his. She curled her fingers between his and held on tight, squeezing a little and smiling at him.

"I like it here," she said, happiness shining in her eyes. "And it smells delicious."

"Not as delicious as you, I'll wager," he said, just loud enough in the burble of noise surrounding them that she heard and blushed a lovely shade of pink.

The look in her eyes said *wicked man,* but the smile on her lips said that she liked him just fine. Ludo sighed and realised that he was happy. How strange life was, that one could be so low, so close to despairing, and then be lifted to such dizzying heights by another.

Their meal came—pork chops and boiled potatoes and good, thick gravy—and Ludo tucked in with gusto, polishing off his serving and ordering another before Bunty was half way through hers.

"Eat up," he chided her. "You need to keep your strength up, my lady."

Puzzled for a moment, she looked up at him.

"Why…?" she began, and then pursed her lips as he chuckled at her.

Once their meal was over, Ludo paid and escorted her outside once more.

"Oh, Ludo, it's snowing," she said in delight, holding out her gloved hand and watching as the tiny flakes settled for a moment before disappearing.

"So it is. I had better take you home and warm you up, then."

She laughed, looking up at him with such an expression of happiness that the earth seemed to pitch beneath his feet and settle anew, as though rearranged and nothing would ever be the same again. The frail, blossoming flame of hope unfurled a little farther inside him, warming him. He stopped in his tracks and she opened her mouth, no doubt to ask why, but Ludo bent his head and kissed her, there in the street, in full view of everyone.

She gave a soft gasp, and for a moment he thought she was cross, but then her mouth tilted up at the edges, a smile for him alone.

"Bunty," he said, his voice suddenly hoarse, trembling with uncertainty but wanting to tell her, to give her the truth of everything he felt. "Bunty, I—"

"Well, well, if it ain't Ludo, and feeling up his light-o'-love in the middle of the street, no less."

Ludo stiffened, his heart jolting in his chest, the familiar sense of panic washing over him at that voice, that vile, awful voice.

"That's my wife you speak of, Bramwell," he said, turning towards the face of his nightmares.

Stupid. He was a grown man, big enough to pick Bramwell up and shake him in one hand, yet somehow he was never a grown man with his big brother. Instead, Ludo found himself reduced to a snivelling child, pissing his pants with terror of what the beast would do next.

"Ah, yes. Heard you got yourself caught in a snare, big, dumb ox that you are. Thinking with your prick as ever, eh?" Bramwell turned those cold, green eyes to Bunty. "And you, you foolish chit, did you think he had his hands on the family money, my sweet? He ain't and won't ever have."

Ludo felt the way she stiffened with indignation, and drew her in, close to his side. He would not let Bramwell hurt her. Surely he could manage that at least. Couldn't he? He felt frozen, his guts churning.

"You heard wrong, my lord. It was a tryst, and one I was eager for, I assure you. Incidentally, I wouldn't touch your money with a ten-foot pole, and neither would Ludo," Bunty said, with all the poise of a queen speaking to a lowly pleb.

Ludo stared at her in awe.

"Ah, a feisty one, and toothsome too," Bramwell said, leering at Bunty in a way that made Ludo long to knock his teeth down his throat.

The hand that wasn't holding Bunty plastered to his side closed into a fist, but he couldn't breathe. Something cold and panicky held him immobile. Years of being locked in cupboards and small spaces, of pranks that had seen him tumbling down stairs or tripped on his face, of myriad little everyday cruelties and bigger ones too made him freeze with terror. Dangling him by his ankles from an upper storey window had been one of Bramwell's favourites until Ludo had become too big to hold. Bramwell hadn't realised his limitations before he'd almost dropped Ludo on his head, mind you.

"No, not in the least feisty, just honest," Bunty said with a thin smile. "You see, I recognise a bully when I see one."

"Ha!" Bramwell seemed genuinely amused by that. "One need not be a bully when a fellow's such a weakling. Don't let all that brawn fool you, my flower. He's a pathetic worm. No, you come see me if it's a man you're wanting, I'll see you right…."

Bramwell raised his hand, as if he would touch Bunty. He reached for her, cruelty in every bone, down to his marrow, and something inside Ludo fractured. Bunty was everything good in his life, a golden gossamer thread, a bright glimmer of hope, of truth and kindness and trust, and he loved… *loved* her. Yet Bramwell reached out as if he had the right to lay his filthy hand on her lovely skin. Ludo reacted. He didn't know what he'd done at first, what exactly had happened, but the next moment Bramwell lay sprawled on the floor, ungainly and ridiculous, his hat having tumbled away into the gutter. Bramwell was gasping, fishlike, his glassy eyes dazed, and he was bleeding like a stuck pig. There had been the crunch of bone, Ludo thought. Bramwell's nose, perhaps? He looked at his fist, a little stunned. He'd done it. After so many years of wishing he had the courage, he'd done it. He had fought so many bigger men—far more dangerous men—and yet Bramwell had always effortlessly reduced him to that terrified child.

No longer.

Ludo turned to look at Bunty, who was beaming at him. She threw her arms about his neck and kissed him.

"Well done!"

He fought the urge to preen, aware he'd not acted as a gentleman, but too relieved to have acted at all to give a damn. He looked back to see Mr Middleton, the family's man of business, helping Bramwell up. He'd not even noticed him before now. That was Middleton all over, though: never noticed, always in the background, quietly smoothing over the difficulties Ludo's loud-mouthed brothers and his devil of a father created. No. Not *his* father. Ludo was none of his, thank God.

Bramwell looked shaken, and older than Ludo remembered. Well, he *was* older, fifteen years older. He'd been the nightmare that had terrorised Ludo once his mother had died. Bramwell and his brother George had been partners in crime, devising ways to torture Ludo with their father's blessing until he was afraid of his own shadow.

"Stay away from my wife," Ludo managed, clutching Bunty's hand.

He drew strength from her, strength enough to look into the eyes that had always made him afraid, but without flinching. Never again would he flinch. He'd fight dragons for Bunty. He could deal with this… this obnoxious, overweight fool. Ludo allowed himself to really look at Bramwell, and saw the paunch, the double chin and bloodshot eyes. He was getting old, old and weak, years of dissipation and cruelty shown plainly on a face that did not understand kindness, tenderness, or compassion. Ludo pitied him.

"I don't want to see you again, Bramwell, and you may tell George to expect the same treatment. Stay away from us. I want none of you, and we certainly have no interest in your money."

He looked at Bunty, saw her eyes shining with admiration, and with belief in him.

"We don't need it," he added.

She smiled at him and squeezed his hand.

Bramwell sent him a look of pure loathing, one hand clutching a handkerchief to his nose, which was bleeding profusely. Middleton, efficient as ever, had hailed a hackney and helped Bramwell inside. He hesitated before moving back to Ludo.

"Come and see me, my lord. As soon as you may. It's important."

Ludo opened his mouth to say he wouldn't go anywhere near anyone associated with his family, but Middleton put a hand out, holding Ludo's arm for a moment. From neat, balding, precise Middleton, this was so extraordinary that Ludo could only stare.

"Please," he said urgently, and then hurried back to the hackney and got in.

***

Ludo was silent as they walked back home, and Bunty did not press him, aware that he needed a little quiet to gather himself. She held tight to his arm, though, so he knew she was with him, supporting him. Once again, she remembered the look on his face when he'd seen his oldest brother. He'd gone the most startling shade of white, his big frame rigid with tension. She'd known then, or at least she suspected she knew what kind of man Bramwell Courtenay, the Earl of Edgmond, was. He was the kind to inflict harm on those weaker than him and take pleasure in it. She could see it at once in those callous eyes, as lacking in feeling as a dead fish. It was in the cruelty of his thin lips, just as much as in his vile words and insinuations. It was in the way she had felt Ludo react, an instinct born of years of abuse at the hands of an older brother.

She imagined Ludo as a boy, all glorious tumbling black curls and big blue eyes, and then two brothers in Bramwell's mould, and....

And the Marquess of Farringdon. Everyone knew of him. Everyone knew of the marquess and his cruelty, his vicious temper and his pride. How must a man like that have felt to have discovered himself a cuckold?

Oh, Ludo.

Her heart broke and she held tighter to his arm. It had been such a shock to see his fear. Ludo was so large, so vital and strong, so powerful. She'd read of his brawling, read of his skill in the boxing ring. One of Jackson's favourites, he was a natural. All that beautiful strength that he had given her so wholeheartedly and with such tenderness, had been driven away with a few words from a man who must have tormented his childhood. She wanted to go back to Bramwell now, this instant, and... and....

Bunty sucked in a breath, startled by the violence of her own thoughts, the anger and the need for retribution. She had never in her life wanted to hurt someone, but... but Bramwell had hurt Ludo. Bramwell had been his big brother, a role that ought to at least be one of camaraderie, if not of protection. And instead....

"Bunty?"

Bunty blinked, looking up at Ludo's appalled face, only then realising her eyes were wet with tears.

"Oh, God, Bunty, I'm so sorry. I should not have let him speak to you so. I... I should have—"

She reached up and pressed a finger to his lips. "You did. You were admirable. I'm so proud of you. Now do open the door and let us go inside. The snow is falling heavier, I think."

Bunty watched as he fumbled for the key, letting them in. He seemed a little lost, uncertain, and she took off his overcoat, guided him to a chair and made him sit down as she stoked the fire back to life and put a kettle on for tea. She hung up wet things and pulled off his boots as the kettle sang. Calmed by routine, she poured tea, putting a cup into his hand, dosed heavily with sugar.

He sipped and she watched him come back to himself. To her. Taking his empty cup, she put it down and sat in his lap. He sighed and wrapped his arms around her, laying his head against her shoulder as she stroked his hair, curling now, damp from the snow despite his hat.

"Tell me," she said.

He did, haltingly at first, and then a tumble of words like water rushing over a cliff's edge, eager for the fall, eager to rid himself of the memories and let them flow away.

Bunty heard it, all of it, stoic, not weeping, though she wanted to. She wanted to sob and rage and howl with fury, but she held it back, certain he would not want that. She held him, though, kissed him when she could no longer bear not to, smothered her anger and turned it into a caress. It was at once just as she had imagined, and far worse. When he was done, she did not move, aware that he was calm now, not wanting to disturb his tranquillity by doing or saying the wrong thing.

"It wasn't all bad," he said, squeezing her fingers.

She blinked hard as his face blurred, touched that he would want to reassure her, when he was the one who had lived it.

"Whilst my mother lived, I was protected and cosseted and loved. I do remember that. She told me about my real father."

"The Italian count?"

He nodded.

"She would not run off with him because she did not want you to endure the scandal, yet she named you Ludovic? Like your father, Ludovico?" She tried to keep the censure from her voice, but failed.

He shrugged, his big shoulders rolling. "At first, she thought she'd got away with it, I think. I think she believed it would be her private joke. Yet it wasn't long before it became clear I was not like my brothers, and the rumours flew. She believed she'd been discreet, yet someone knew. Someone always knows. She took me away then, ran away, more like."

"Where did you go?"

Ludo smiled. "She had a house in Kent. Hers, not Father's. He could not take it from her. Some legal quirk. He tried to get around it, but her mother had been a canny soul, I think. Anyway, she took us there, and we were happy."

"Until she died."

Pain flickered in his eyes, and Bunty wanted to never see such an expression again. She vowed she would do anything she could to prevent it.

"Yes. I was eight. Then... Then it was not good at all. Not for a long time. Not..." He reached up and cupped her face, and she wondered at the gentleness of this man, who'd had so little of it in his life. "Not until you."

Bunty turned into his touch and kissed his palm, holding his hand there with her own.

"It is the strangest thing," he said, a wondering tone to his voice. "To think he has frightened me so these many years when... when he's nothing. He's less than nothing. A vain, vile nothing of a man. He has money and power, and yet he's...."

"Pathetic," Bunty said firmly, disgust in every syllable. "Preying on those weaker than himself. He's no man, Ludo. Not like you. He does not deserve a moment more of your attention, and I should like it very much if you never thought of him ever again, but... but if you do, if you want to tell me more... anything. I shall always listen."

Ludo tipped his head back and stared at her.

"I don't understand it," he said, almost to himself. "I don't understand what I did. How did I manage it? How did I convince you to marry me?"

Bunty did not consider that a question worthy of an answer, as it was far too obvious, so she kissed him instead, and he seemed to like that well enough.

Chapter 6

"Wherein the final piece of the puzzle reveals a lovely picture."

14th December 1820. London.

Ludo awoke early. It was barely dawn, just a faint smudge of daylight creeping around the curtains. Bunty sighed and snuggled closer to him, and Ludo smiled. Lucky bastard. She was warm and soft and... and rather astonishing. He'd tried to untangle everything it was he felt for her, but it had all been so sudden, and yet a creeping thing that he'd been vaguely aware of for years. He'd always held his breath when he'd caught sight of her in a crowd, on a street, or at the theatre. It had been like glimpsing a dream, something lovely and so impossible you could not hope to hold on to it, aware that it was never to be real, never to be yours. He tightened his grip on her lush curves—which were reassuringly tangible and mouth–watering—as she sighed and stretched. His feelings rose in a mess of untidy bafflement. He did not understand why she had protected him so fiercely when he'd been so obviously, pathetically weak. He did not know why she should smile at him with happiness sparkling in her eyes when he'd done so little to deserve it. God, he'd taken her from an opulent home and installed her in this dingy place, and yet she looked at him like... like she was *glad*.

The tangle in his chest was woven so tight he suspected he would never unravel it, but in the end it resolved itself into one bright, shining truth, so obvious it was undeniable. Not that he wanted to deny it. He wanted to shout it from the rooftops, but he did not think she would like that. Besides, he needed to tell her first.

She stirred again, with a flutter of dark eyelashes, and her lovely eyes were warm and soft, hazy with sleep, and then with a hotter emotion as her gaze settled on him. Oh, he liked that look.

"Good morning," she murmured, giving a contented sigh of pleasure.

Ludo shifted down the bed until they were eye to eye.

"Good morning, beautiful."

She made a little harrumphing sound and put a hand up to her hair, wincing. "You are an odd creature, to enjoy such a sight."

"No. I am your husband, and right about all things. I do not care that your hair looks like a bird has nested in it. You *are* beautiful: quite astoundingly lovely."

There was a helpless laugh that made his heart kick about behind his ribs, and then she looked up at him.

"You *are* an odd creature, but I like you very much. I like your compliments, and I love waking up with you."

"I love you, Bunty."

Her mouth fell open, and Ludo sat up as she lay there, gazing at him.

"I do. I love you."

She blinked hard, her eyes glittering, and Ludo panicked as a tear escaped.

Oh. Oh, no. Ought he not have said that? Was it too soon? Should he have waited?

"Oh, Bunty… I…."

He did not know what to say. He could not… *would* not take it back. The truth of it had settled inside him, weighty and honest, and he did not want to deny it.

Only… only if she did not want it….

Her soft hands reached for him, pulling his head down. She kissed him, murmuring against his lips.

"Love you. I love you, Ludo. You've made me so happy."

Oh, thank Christ for that.

He kissed her back, enthusiastic now, eager to make her happier still. As a husband he might not have been up to much—not yet, anyway, though he had plans, lots of plans—but this… this he could do. This he could do very well, thank you very much.

So he did. Several times.

***

It took a great deal of persuading to get Ludo out of bed, more to get him out of the house, particularly when he realised where she wanted to go.

"He said it was important, Ludo."

Ludo huffed, grumbling as he pulled on his greatcoat.

Bunty hoped her instincts were correct, and that this visit to the family's man of business would not cause him further upset. She had seen the distaste in Mr Middleton's eyes when his employer had come upon them yesterday. In fact, she believed loathing was closer to what she had seen there. It had been hidden beneath a façade of professionalism and icy civility once he'd bent to help the earl to his feet, from where Ludo had sent him sprawling, but it had unmistakeably been there.

To her relief, they would not need to visit any of the family homes, for Mr Middleton also kept an office in the city.

"Well, if we must, I ought to call in and see to some business of my own on the way," said Ludo, his tone suggesting he was still unenthusiastic about the idea, but accepting at least.

"Of course," she said brightly, tying her bonnet.

She looked up as he moved before her and tweaked the bow, before leaning down and kissing her.

"Gorgeous," he said, leaving her giddy and happily dazed with nothing more than a word and a peck on the lips.

***

Bunty kicked her heels in the hallway of the large red brick building, a little irritated to have been abandoned, but not wanting to pry. Men were funny about matters involving money, and Ludo was obviously very much on his dignity about the state of his finances. Still, her curiosity burned, and she dared to wander down the hallway a bit and peek into the room at the end. A huge printing press was set up here, and the smell of ink hung heavy on the air.

"I knew you'd not be able to resist."

Bunty spun around to see Ludo watching her.

"Oh. Well, no. I'm sorry. Only I had nothing to do and I was curious. Is this part of your business? Printing?"

"In a way," he said. He seemed rather tense, anxious and yet also pleased.

"Did your meeting go well?"

He nodded, turning this hat around and around in his hand.

"It did, better than I expected. We've…." He laughed, a glint of astonishment in his eyes. "We've made some money. Not… Not a huge amount, but more than we'd expected."

"Well, that's marvellous," she said, meaning it. "But how, Ludo? Won't you tell me?"

He hesitated. She moved towards him and took his hand, aware that he was nervous, but uncertain why.

"Promise you won't laugh."

Bunty stared up at him. "Why on earth would I laugh at something that makes money?"

He ran a hand through his hair, making it stick up in a riot of thick dark curls. Bunty reached up on her toes and enjoyed the miraculous delight of smoothing it back into place.

"Well," he said, staring down at her. "Oh, come along. I'll show you."

He tugged at her hand and Bunty hurried beside him as he strode down the corridor and up a flight of stairs. He opened a door, guiding her into a cramped, dingy office. Weak daylight filtered in through the grubby windows, and the place needed a good sweep, but Bunty strove to ignore that, too curious about what he wanted to show her.

He closed the door and tapped his hat on his thigh a couple of times before clearing his throat. "Have you ever seen those dissection puzzles? I had one as a boy. Well, what was left of one. Half the pieces were missing by the time it came to me, but it was a map of the world pasted onto board and cut up into sections. It was supposed to teach geography, and it did, rather cleverly. I always thought it would be more fun if there were other things to put back together, though. Pictures, for example."

"What sort of pictures?" she asked, more than surprised at his words.

He shrugged, a little diffident, and then gestured to a table where there were a dozen or more boxes stacked. Bunty moved to the table and, as he seemed to be waiting for her to do so, lifted the lid on the box nearest her. There were a jumble of pieces inside and she tipped them onto the table.

"Oh," she said, enchanted to see what he meant. Putting aside her reticule, she organised the pieces, putting them back together to make a picture of a smug-looking cat, his paw holding down the tail of a mouse. The poor mouse was yanking at his tail like fury, trying to get free. "Oh, Ludo, it's marvellous. A child would love this."

Ludo grinned at her.

"That one is for a younger child. There's a dog, too, and a rabbit. Then here, these are for older children." He tipped over another box, scattering more pieces, smaller and more complex this time. "There's a farmyard scene, and a knight fighting a dragon so far."

Bunty exclaimed with delight and said nothing at all for some time, deep in concentration until she had completed the farmyard scene, complete with a pretty cottage, a milkmaid and chickens and ducks, sheep and cows.

"It's beautiful. What a clever artist you have to draw such beautiful pictures too."

She looked up to see his face filled with pleasure. "Well, the pen drawings are printed out so we can reproduce them in numbers, but then they are hand-painted so they're colourful."

Bunty stared at the puzzle a little longer, considering, studying the way the light glimmered on the duck pond and the sunlight glittered on the puddles in the cobbled yard, as if it had just rained.

"These are the originals?" she guessed, looking up at him.

Ludo nodded. "The painting on the ones we sell are less detailed, as it takes too long, but still very good quality. We've some marvellous painters working with us."

"Yes," Bunty agreed, nodding. "You do."

"You like them, then?" he asked, and she heard the eagerness in his voice.

"I think they're wonderful. Any child would be delighted to receive such a gift. Goodness, *I* would be delighted. They're marvellous, Ludo."

Bunty squealed as he swept her up, spun her around, and then kissed her soundly.

"*You're* marvellous," he said, and she could see happiness shining in his eyes.

Her heart lurched, knowing she had done that. She kissed him and then pushed him away with a laugh, returning the puzzles she'd made back to their boxes. As she put the last lid back on the box she frowned, tracing her finger over the words, *John Cooper's Dissected Puzzles.*

"This was your idea, wasn't it, Ludo? Your creation?"

Ludo nodded. "Yes."

"Then why isn't your name on the box. Who is John Cooper?"

"John is the printer, my business partner. Be reasonable, love. Who in their right mind would buy something for a child created by Lascivious Lord Courtenay?"

He laughed, but she thought there was regret in the sound.

"I suppose so," she said, not liking the truth of his words. "It's not fair, though, when it was your idea."

Rather more than his idea, she suspected.

Ludo moved closer to her and lifted her chin, kissing her. "You know. That's all I care about. Now come along, my love, and let us get the tedious part of the day over with. I've no doubt Middleton will put me in a wretched temper, so I shall leave it to you to cheer me up once we're done."

He winked at her to show he didn't blame her for dragging him to see the man, and Bunty followed him out to find a hackney.

***

Mr Middleton's office was every bit as neat and precise as the man himself. He was small of stature, balding, and with a round face which seemed rounder still as he peered owlishly out from behind thick spectacles. He took them off, cleaning the lenses with care, and surreptitiously glancing at Ludo who was pacing the elegant room like a caged lion, tension rolling off his large frame with every move.

"Ludo, do come and sit down," Bunty said, patting the chair beside her, aware that his prowling was making Mr Middleton nervous.

He folded his arms, scowling, and for a moment Bunty worried he'd balk and tell Middleton to bloody well get on with it. She could see the desire to do so burning in his eyes. She patted the seat again and he sighed, moving to sit beside her with a glower. Bunty reached for his hand and he curled his fingers around hers.

"Thank you for coming, my lord," Middleton said, replacing his spectacles. "I... I admit I was uncertain you would come but, for once, I believe I can do you some good."

"You mean unlike that time when you told me my father had cut me out of his will?"

Middleton blanched and Bunty squeezed his hand.

"Mr Middleton was only doing his job, Ludo. It was not his choice."

Middleton sent her a look of profound gratitude and nodded. "Quite so, my lord. I was sorry to do it, and for any other... er... unpleasantness that has passed through my hands over the years."

Ludo snorted but said nothing.

"Bearing that in mind, I beg you to remember that your father is my employer and that he strictly forbade me to give you any details of... of the inheritance your mother left you."

"Inheritance?" Ludo echoed, sounding stunned. "But there was nothing. Father always took great delight in reminding me I had nothing of hers...."

He broke off and Bunty firmed her grip on his hand.

"That was untrue, I regret to say," Middleton said with a heavy sigh. "Though it would not have been yours until now, until you took a wife. Those were the terms of the will."

Mr Middleton reached down beside him and lifted a box, placing it on the table before him. "Firstly, there are these personal effects which your mother wished you to have."

Bunty watched Ludo, saw his throat working, saw the moment he gathered his courage and reached for the box. He placed it carefully on his lap and lifted the lid.

Inside were two small paintings. One was of his mother as a young woman, a beautiful smiling portrait with vivid blue eyes and soft brown curls.

"You have her eyes," Bunty said, hearing her voice quaver.

Ludo blinked hard and nodded, handing her the painting to look beneath.

"Oh," he said.

Here was a painting of a man. A big, rugged, pirate of a man, with thick black curls and dark, laughing eyes, a full sensuous mouth, and an air of disreputable charm.

"Your father," Middleton said, smiling. "I believe there are details of where he might be contacted, should you wish to do so?"

"He's still alive?" Ludo said, clearly astonished. "But Bramwell said—" He cursed and shook his head. "Idiot."

"Aren't you glad you came?" Bunty asked gently, watching his face.

"I am," he said, staring at the portrait of his father, of a man who bore a striking resemblance to Ludo. He reached for his mother's portrait, and Bunty felt her heart constrict as he touched a reverent finger to her lovely face. "Thank you, Middleton. I... I cannot tell you how happy I am to have these. I'm grateful."

Middleton returned a look full of regret. "I am only happy to have brought you something pleasant for a change, my lord."

"Not your fault," Ludo said gruffly, putting the paintings back in the box with care. He stood and held his hand out to the man. "Well, if that's all, I'll bid you—"

"Oh! No, my lord, that is not all."

Ludo frowned at him. "It isn't?"

Middleton shook his head, his eyes glimmering with amusement. "No, Lord Courtenay. There is the matter of your mother's house, and a bequest of... let me see, with interest... yes, nine thousand, eight hundred and twenty-seven pounds.

Ludo sat down again with such a crash Bunty feared for the chair.

"H-House?" he said faintly. "Nine thousand...?"

"Nine thousand, eight hundred and twenty-seven pounds, ten shillings and sixpence, if you wish the precise figure," Middleton repeated helpfully.

"Breathe, Ludo," Bunty said, reaching for his hand again, as he'd gone a rather odd colour.

He clutched at her hand so tightly she almost protested.

"Where is the house?" Bunty said, hoping it was Ludo's childhood home.

"In Kent, Lady Courtenay. I understand it has been in Lord Courtenay's mother's family for generations. It is in good order, having had caretakers look after it in the interim. I took the liberty of asking them to prepare for your arrival, having assumed you would wish to visit the property."

"The caretakers," Ludo asked, his voice hoarse. "Who?"

"A Mr and Mrs Widdershins."

"Widdy," he said, audibly choked now. "Oh, good Lord. I never... I never imagined...." He turned to Bunty, his eyes shining with emotion. "A home, Bunty. We have a home. *My* home!"

"Oh, Ludo, I'm so happy for you." Bunty turned back to Mr Middleton, hardly able to get the words out. "Thank you."

The man looked a little overcome himself, but nodded, obviously pleased.

Ludo stood and held out his hand to Mr Middleton, who was now looking a little stunned, no doubt used to less than polite treatment at the hands of Ludo's family.

"Thank you, Middleton. Thank you so much, and I do understand... why you didn't tell me before."

Middleton shook his hand firmly. "I have wished to these many years, my lord, only...."

"No need to explain," Ludo said kindly. "He's your employer. I understand, truly."

Middleton frowned, looking extremely displeased at this fact.

"He is, and I am not in a position to consider retirement, not with five daughters still unmarried," he added with a sigh. "However, should you ever be in a position to... to...."

He flushed then, such an extraordinary sight against his serious visage that Bunty's eyebrows rose.

"You would like to come and work for Lord Courtenay?" she guessed.

Ludo stared at her in astonishment and then looked back to Middleton. "You're not serious? You'd leave my father's employ for *mine*?"

"In a heartbeat," Middleton said calmly.

Ludo's incredulity made Bunty's chest hurt. He'd truly had no idea that there was anyone who would believe in him. Yet anyone who had been in his company for any length of time must have been able to see the goodness that shone from him, the honour and integrity.

Ludo frowned, considering this. "Middleton, I have a business venture that is showing signs of promise. It needs a firm hand, a good business brain to get it off the ground. I also have... nine thousand, eight hundred, and—"

"Twenty-seven pounds, ten shillings and sixpence," Middleton supplied for him.

"Precisely." Ludo nodded. "Can I afford you?"

Middleton grinned at him. "I believe that you can, my lord."

Chapter 7

"Wherein a house in the country."

14th December 1820. London.

They returned home and began packing at once as Ludo was beside himself with excitement. He gave his landlady notice on his rooms and arranged for a carriage to collect them and their luggage at nine the following morning. Packing didn't take long. Besides a wardrobe that certainly rivalled Bunty's for quantity, and most certainly for style, Ludo had few belongings. Bunty had not yet had the belongings which were a part of her dowry sent over, as Ludo's rooms simply had not the space for them. She was cross, in fact, that her parents had still not visited once since her marriage. The only word she'd had were a few tearful letters from her mother and a rather sternly worded note from her father, which gruffly reminded her she could return home at any time, should she come to realise the gravity of the mistake she'd made. Bunty could not blame them for their fears, but she could blame them for being ashamed and not coming to visit her.

She therefore took great delight in writing and telling them both how blissfully happy she was, how Ludo's business had the makings of a terrific success, and how they were about to move into their new home in the country, where Ludo would keep her in fine style, thank you very much. The letter included a pointed reminder that Papa had not announced their marriage, and a firm suggestion that he do so, at once. She did not invite them for Christmas. She would invite them soon, naturally, but not yet. Perhaps Easter, but only if they swore to be polite to her husband.

Bunty looked around to see if there was anything left to pack, finding only the two lovely paintings on the wall. Smiling, she moved towards them and took the one of the elegant house off the wall. She looked up as Ludo came in from outside, bringing the scent of cold air with him and brushing snow from his hair. He ran to her and swept her up, kissing her hard and making her squeal with the press of his cold lips and icy hands upon her warm skin.

"Warm me up, wife. I'm chilled to the marrow."

"Eek! Get off me, you're freezing," she complained, though half-heartedly.

He stilled, looking at the picture she had clung to valiantly during his boisterous entrance.

"That's it," he said, smiling at her. "That's home."

Bunty nodded, thrilled that she'd been correct.

"It's so beautiful, Ludo. I can't wait to live there, with you and… and you painted it, didn't you? And all the pictures for the puzzles. Why ever didn't you tell me?" she exclaimed crossly as he gave a sheepish nod. "I'm so proud of you. Imagine having an artist for a husband!"

"You don't mind?" he asked, rubbing the back of his neck and looking awkward.

Bunty stared at him, perplexed. "Why would I mind?"

He shrugged. "Oh, I don't know. It's not very… manly."

"Don't be ridiculous, whoever…?" She sighed and shook her head. "Never mind. Darling, if ever something as stupid as that thought crosses your mind again, would you just investigate the source of it before you believe it? I feel confident supposing it was something Farringdon, or one of your ghastly brothers told you. Am I correct?"

Ludo frowned, considering this and then his face cleared. "Yes, by God. How—"

Bunty pressed a finger to his lips. "Did it never cross your mind that all the great artists are men? Women don't get a look in."

Ludo huffed. "Well, obviously, but that's hardly what this is. This is dabbling with watercolours, which is exactly what young ladies do, and your Great-Aunt Mary."

"I don't have a Great-Aunt Mary."

He rolled his eyes. "You know what I mean."

"Yes. I do, and you're wrong. Ludo, you're not dabbling. I may be biased, but I do have an eye for a good painting. I met Henry Barbour once and he told me so. What's more, I believe these are more than good. I think they're excellent, and I know you ought to take it seriously."

"You met Henry Barbour?" Ludo's eyes had lit with awe, and he appeared to have completely disregarded everything else she'd said.

"I did, yes. Father is a distant cousin of the Marquess of Winterbourne, who is one of Mr Barbour's closest friends. We were there one summer, and he introduced me."

"He's not the slightest bit mad, is he?"

Bunty shook her head at once.

"Goodness, no. Very shy, rather, and somewhat eccentric, to be sure. He dislikes people on the whole, but he was charming and spoke to me at length about his work, and about some of the others I'd seen at the Royal Academy's summer exhibition. Indeed, I think I should show him some of yours. Perhaps I shall send one to him," she mused.

All the colour drained from Ludo's face. "Oh, no. Not on your life. He's... he's a *genius.* You'll not go sending my paltry offerings to show him."

Bunty sighed and set his painting aside with care before moving back to him. She wrapped her arms about his waist and stared up at him.

"I'm fat," she said baldly. "I'm fat and ungainly, and too tall."

His face darkened with fury.

"And I'm the Queen of Sheba!" he retorted. "What the devil has made you say so? You're gorgeous, Bunty. Surely you know I can't keep my bloody hands off you? I've been half in love with you for... for *years,* wishing and hoping such a beautiful creature could be mine."

Bunty swallowed down the emotion that made her throat feel tight on hearing those impassioned words. Instead, she reached up and touched his cheek.

"You're an artist, Ludo. You're a clever, talented man, and you will be a great success. I am so proud of you. I believe in you. The only thing left to do is believe in yourself."

"That was a dirty trick," he grumbled, but he pulled her close and she smiled up at him.

"It made my point, though. Other people have always given me their opinions, far too freely, and I always believed them. Yet, you make me see they were wrong, terribly, cruelly wrong. Let me do the same for you, love. That wretch, Farringdon, your brothers, they all made you feel worthless, and that's so far from the truth."

He let out a breath and nodded.

"Very well," he said, still a little gruff. "But it will be some time before I have the courage to show anything to Henry Barbour, let me assure you."

"That's all right. We have plenty of time."

***

The journey to Russell House was cold and tedious, but neither Ludo nor Bunty complained. Buoyed by excitement and distracted by each other, the time passed pleasantly as Ludo invented ways to keep Bunty warm. He was very good at it.

They worried as the snow fell with increasing enthusiasm: large, soft flakes tumbling from the white sky overhead and laying still and pristine over the beautiful landscape.

"How lovely it is," Bunty said, staring out of the window.

"It is. It makes me wish I had my paints to hand but, all the same, I wish it would leave off until we're sat in front of a warm fire."

"We'll get there." Bunty ducked back under his arm and luxuriated in his warmth. Her husband was better than any hot brick for keeping warm on a long journey.

Despite being slowed by the snow, they arrived at midday. Ludo jumped out of the carriage, reaching back to help Bunty, and then gazed up at the house in wonder.

"My word, but it's lovely. I feel like I'm dreaming. Is it really ours?"

"It is," Bunty said, enjoying the pleasure in his eyes and his obvious happiness.

"It's smaller than I remember," he said with a laugh. "In my memories it's a vast, cavernous place, but it is every bit as beautiful."

Bunty laughed. "Well, I don't think it's shrunk, love, more that you've grown. It is beautiful, though."

It was. A seven hundred-year-old medieval hall house overlooking the rolling Kentish countryside, the place was graceful and ancient. Elegant arched windows and an arched front door gave it a romantic feel, especially now, with its long roof dusted with snow and the chimneys coiling smoke into the sky and promising a warm welcome.

The front door opened as they walked towards it, and an older couple appeared. The lady was short and squat with iron grey hair, and a fierce expression that softened when she laid eyes on Ludo. She reached for her apron and pressed it to her mouth to muffle a little cry of delight.

"Widdy?" Ludo said, incredulous even though he'd known the old housekeeper would still be here. "Is that really you?"

"*Oh*," the woman said, trying valiantly to curtsey and not to cry, nor to run and hug Ludo as she clearly wished to do. "Oh, welcome home, my lord."

To Bunty's delight, Ludo had no such restraint and gave her a hug, swift and enthusiastic.

"You've not changed a bit," he said, delighted and earning himself a snort of disbelief. "Nor you, Mr Widdershins. I feel like a boy again."

"Ah, and we have missed you, my lord. You and your Mama both, God rest her soul. My poor Agnes was heartbroken when they took you away. Never forgot you, she never. Always said a prayer for you on Sunday and hoped you'd marry and come back home again."

Ludo swallowed hard and hugged Mrs Widdershins again, and this time she burst into tears.

"Oh. I knew you was unhappy," she wailed. "I knew that horrid man didn't treat you right, or else how would such a good boy have gone off and been so very wicked?"

She blushed and clamped her mouth shut, realising too late she'd just insulted the marquess and Ludo both, but Ludo only laughed.

"No, don't stop there, Widdy. You're right, of course. About all of it. I was a devilish fellow, to be sure, but I am home now, thank God, and I mean to behave, I promise. I must thank you, though, for never forgetting me and for keeping me in your prayers, and certainly for keeping the place so beautifully. It's just how I remember it. And now, before I am accused of forgetting my manners entirely… this lovely creature is my wife. Bunty, please meet Mr and Mrs Widdershins. Mr and Mrs Widdershins, my wife, Lady Courtenay."

***

Ludo was as enthusiastic as a boy whilst Widdy—as she insisted Bunty address her—showed them around the house. At every turn, Ludo exclaimed as some memory returned to him of his darling mama and the happy times they'd had here together. Bunty was overcome with joy for him, and so relieved that his memories had in no way been diminished or overshadowed by what had come next. He clearly felt no ill will towards his mother for the situation in which she had left him, despite how awful it had been. To Bunty, this showed just how good-hearted and generous her husband was and, impossibly, she felt herself fall more in love with him with every passing moment.

Bunty watched as he laughed with Widdy, recalling an incident when he'd eaten an entire tray of jam tarts and then sworn blind that he hadn't despite the sticky evidence around his person that called him a liar.

"Ah, but you was sorry for it, and begged my pardon so nicely," Widdy said, dabbing at her eyes with her apron. "I couldn't be cross with you."

Smiling, Bunty wondered if the Ratched sisters were having as lovely a time as she was, and if they would ever be so happy. How strange that their avaricious plans had turned out so wonderfully for her and Ludo. As it was Christmas, or very near, Bunty sent them a silent thank you, for without them, she might never have married Ludo, and that would have been a tragedy.

Finally, Widdy showed them to their own room, the one that had once belonged to Ludo's mother.

"Well, I'll leave you be for a while, as I no doubt you're eager for me to do, if I know anything about newlyweds. There'll be a hot meal waiting for you in an hour, should you wish for it, but I shan't bat an eyelid if you don't. I'll leave tea and biscuits outside the door in the meantime, but I'll not disturb you again, my lord. Ring for me if you need aught, though."

"Thank you, Widdy," Ludo said, sending her such a warm smile that poor Widdy looked quite flustered. "For such a lovely welcome. I know we shall be very happy here."

"Ah, well. All is as it ought to be at last, my lord," Widdy said, dipping a curtsey before she left them alone and closed the door behind her.

Bunty watched as Ludo moved to the dressing table, touching perfume bottles and silver-backed brushes that must have belonged to his mother with reverent fingers. He lifted one of the crystal bottles and took out the stopper, lifting it to his nose, and smiled. Placing the bottle back with care, he stood by the window and looked out. The light was fading now, twilight settling upon the snow and leaving the landscape hushed and silent. Bunty moved to stand beside him, and he slid his arm about her waist, pulling her close.

"Over that way is Sedlescombe and Battle Abbey, and that way to Hastings. In the summer, we can go to the beach and you can sea bathe. Pevensey Bay is over there, where William the Conqueror landed. There was always a lot of society to be had here, too. A good community, or at least my mother found it so. I'm afraid you may struggle there, what with my black reputation to overcome."

"Nonsense," Bunty said briskly, not wanting anything to spoil his good humour, though there was truth in his words. "Soon enough, they'll see that you've turned over a new leaf and are a good husband and a wonderful man, and until then I am more than content to keep you all to myself."

"Are you?" he asked softly, touching her cheek with a fingertip. "For I don't doubt the rumours are flying already. The neighbourhood will be bracing itself for wild parties and tales of scandal and debauchery."

Bunty snorted.

"Well, they must content themselves with my scandal, and how I trapped the wicked Lord Courtenay into marriage and tamed his wild heart. That should entertain them through Christmas at least." She moved closer to him and laid her head on his chest, hearing the reassuring thud of his heart. "And yes, you daft creature. I am in no need of society just yet. You are all I want for Christmas."

"I have always hated Christmas," he said his voice low. "Since mother died, at least. We had wonderful Christmases here. The house was filled with greenery and Widdy cooked up a storm. Mother helped her, too. She liked stirring the plum pudding, and I always put the charms in."

"Then let us have a Christmas like that," Bunty said, excitement bubbling through her at the idea. Christmas with her parents had always been a bit dull. It had been a blessing when her friend Freddie had been with them to add some fun to the proceedings. "We'll have a wonderful celebration, just as you did when you were a boy. We'll fill the house with food and laughter, and it will be the best Christmas ever. I can make you love it again, Ludo, I'm sure. With a little help, at least."

"I already do," he said, laughing now. "I love you, Bunty. My word, I love you so much I get these moments of sheer terror when I'm afraid I'll wake up and discover I dreamed it all."

Bunty stared at him, so touched by his words she could not speak for a moment.

"I'm no dream, Ludo," she said, pulling his head down for a kiss. She pulled back, whispering the words against his mouth. "I'll prove it to you."

***

Ludo's breath caught as Bunty pushed his coat from his shoulders, allowing it to fall to the floor in a heap before reaching for his waistcoat buttons. He'd meant what he'd said. Everything that had happened since he'd accepted that note had brought him such joy he lived in terror of losing it, of waking and finding it a dream, or of something crashing down upon him that would ruin everything. Yet, looking into Bunty's eyes and seeing her certainty, her confidence in him, he knew now that he was worrying for nothing. This was no dream. This wonderful woman, this home, this future… they were all his. He did not doubt that there would be challenges ahead. There would be difficulties, good days and bad days, for that was life and no one could escape its vagaries and quirks, but he could face it now. Such a short time ago, the world had looked bleak and lonely, and his efforts to change his life had seemed like climbing a mountain with one arm behind his back. Not now. Now he felt he could face anything if Bunty was beside him, and she was. She always would be.

She'd made short work of his waistcoat and had flung his cravat across the room with a wicked grin. He watched, delighted by the anticipation in her eyes as she tugged his shirt from his breeches, and slid her hands under the fabric.

"Christ, your hands are cold!"

Ludo sucked in a breath as goosebumps chased over his skin, but she only laughed at him.

"Wicked creature," he murmured with affection. "Just see how I've corrupted you."

She nodded, a mischievous glint in her eyes. "Indeed you have, my lord. Just think of all the dreadful things I've learned these past days in your company."

"And nights," he added gravely. "Don't forget the nights."

"Oh, Ludo," she said, her voice trembling with laughter. "I could never forget the nights."

She made him strip off the shirt, and then stood for a long moment, staring at his chest in a way that made Ludo feel like king of the world. He watched as she bit her lip, considering, and then moved towards him and rubbed her face over his chest like a cat, her hands caressing his skin as she sighed happily. He thought perhaps she might purr.

"Oh, I've wanted to do that for an age," she said, looking up as he quirked an eyebrow at her. "You're just so…."

"Hairy?"

"Well, yes, but… big and hot and… cuddly."

"Cuddly?" he repeated doubtfully. "I'm not a kitten."

She snorted at that. "Certainly not, though you rather make me feel like one, which is lovely."

He grinned at her, aware he must look smug, but the expression was swiftly wiped from his face as he realised she'd undone the fall on his trousers and was getting to her knees. Her fingers brushed through the trail of hair that arrowed down his belly to the thick thatch from which his arousal strained, begging for attention.

"I found a book when I was packing, Ludo," she said conversationally. "I'd never seen anything like it."

"Oh?" Ludo said, not paying much attention, not when her mouth was so close, her breath a teasing whisper of warmth over his taut skin.

"It had pictures."

"Did it?" he murmured, before his mind snagged on the only book he had with pictures. "Oh!"

"Oh, indeed," she said, though to his relief she did not sound disgusted, or cross, rather amused and curious.

"It was most… illuminating."

Yes. Yes. Yes. Yes, please. His brain kept up an internal monologue as she trailed a fingertip along the crease at the top of his thigh, making him shiver.

She leaned closer and her tongue darted out, giving him an experimental lick, and Ludo groaned. She did it again, and he held his breath. With excruciating tenderness, she took him into her mouth and sucked gently. He felt dizzy.

"You like that?" she asked, pleased.

Ludo whimpered.

There was a surprisingly naughty chuckle, and Ludo gave himself over to the most exquisite torture of his life as his wife practised the art of driving him out of his mind. She was a quick study, and it was an embarrassingly short time before his body grew tight, his mind blank and emptied of any thought except the pleasure she gave him.

"B-Bunty," he said, trying to force her name out, to warn her, but his lust-addled brain could not form words. Ludo gave a hoarse cry and sank his hands into her hair, too far gone to stop, to do anything but give in to the orgasm that rolled through him with the force of a tidal wave.

It took him a long moment to come back to himself, leaning on the wall beside him to keep himself upright, for his knees felt ready to buckle. Dazed, he focused on his wife with difficulty, but did not miss the smug expression that curved her lush mouth as she looked up at him from under her lashes.

"My word," Ludo managed, wondering if he might sit down for a moment. "I've created a monster."

Bunty snorted and covered her mouth with the back of her hand, no doubt to cover up her delighted smile at having brought him practically to his knees.

"Don't make out like you're sorry," she said, grinning at him.

Ludo gave in. He sat heavily down in the nearest chair and quickly divested himself of breeches and boots. He turned a wicked expression on his wife and shook his head. "Oh, no. Not the least bit sorry, love, but... turnabout is fair play."

Bunty, correctly interpreting the look in his eyes, scrambled to her feet with a little shriek as Ludo lunged for her and swept her up into his arms and over one shoulder. Feeling rather like a caveman returning home with his spoils, he dumped her on the bed, where she bounced invitingly on the mattress before he climbed over her.

"L-Ludo," she said, wagging a warning finger at her. "If you m-make me scream, I'll never be able to leave this room, I'll be so mortified...."

"I always make you scream," he retorted, making short work of the buttons on her bodice. "And I can live with that. There seem to be advantages to keeping you in my bed at all hours."

"I'll never be able to look Mrs Widdershins in the eye again. Nor her husband!" she said, covering her face with her hands.

"You'll get over it," Ludo said placidly. "And the rest of the household will just have to get used to it. I may be married, but I have a reputation to uphold."

"Oh, you're—"

"Dreadful," he supplied for her, giving a happy sigh as he exposed her lovely breasts. "Wicked, depraved, utterly reprehensible...."

"Marvellous," Bunty said closing her eyes, a blissful curve to her lips. "The best, *best* husband anywhere in the world... ever."

Ludo cupped her breasts. *You lucky bastard*, he thought, grinning.

"So... you do want me to make you scream, then?" he asked, all innocence.

Bunty cracked open one eye. "Well, obviously. What are you waiting for, Christmas?"

Ludo gave a bark of laughter and shook his head. "Certainly not, love. I am yours to command. So... prepare yourself."

He flung her skirts over her head and wondered how his heart could contain everything he felt as Bunty laughed, and then squealed. She laughed louder still when he pressed a kiss to her stomach, then blew a wet raspberry against her skin. She squirmed and wriggled, and Ludo stared down at her in wonder.

"I love you," he said, serious for just a moment. "And this will be the best Christmas ever."

Bunty shook her head, smiling up at him, her dark eyes filled with adoration.

"No. Only the first of many best evers," she said.

Ludo nodded, seeing the certainty in her eyes and believing it.

"Our first best ever, then. The first of many," he said.

Bunty nodded, and he moved up the bed to kiss her tenderly.

"I love you too, by the way," she said, stroking his face. "In case you were wondering."

"I wasn't," he said, because he knew now, because he believed he was loved, and wanted, and belonged. "But don't ever stop telling me."

He kissed her again, long and slow, and then sat up, staring down at her with a devilish smile.

"Now then, where was I?"

"Making me scream?" Bunty suggested.

Ludo nodded gravely. "Ah, yes. Husbandly duties. Let's see if we can melt all the snow on the roof, shall we?"

Ludo settled back to his work and, whilst they might not have melted *all* the snow, he certainly made his wife scream, and laugh, and love him all the more.

Epilogue

"Wherein there are roses at Christmas."

Five years later...

24th December 1825. Russell House, Kent.

Bunty looked around the dining room with satisfaction. The silver and crystal glittered in the light of the Yule candle that Ludo had lit for her at sunset, as tradition demanded. Her parents were here, having long since come to terms with her wedding Ludo. That their daughter's marriage was a success was something the most cynical of critics would have been hard pressed to deny. Ludo's business had gone from strength to strength, in no small part due to Bunty suggesting they give away some of the puzzles to the most elevated members of the *ton*. Ludo had been sceptical, remarking wryly that they were supposed to sell the things, not give them away, or he'd be bankrupt in short order. However, the tactic had worked marvellously, as those mamas who saw the likes of the Marchioness of Winterbourne's children playing happily with such a toy rushed out to get one for their own little darlings.

Ludo had also finally given in and allowed Bunty to send one of his paintings to Henry Barbour. The response from the man himself had been no surprise to Bunty, who had long been aware of her husband's many talents, but had stunned Ludo. To have such an acclaimed artist so thoroughly endorse his work had been the boost to his confidence he had needed, and he had agreed to submit a piece to the Royal Academy's summer exhibition. If Bunty had been any prouder, she would have crowed.

This Christmas they had a house full, having persuaded Mr and Mrs Middleton and their youngest daughter to come and stay. Mr Middleton's eldest four girls were now married and off his hands, and the man's relief was palpable. So only young Betsy remained. She was almost nineteen and would likely spend the entire holiday making sheep's eyes at Ludo, but Bunty could hardly blame the girl. Besides which, it would do her no good, for Ludo only had eyes for Bunty. It seemed extraordinary, especially after five years and three children, but he could find no fault with her and loved her to her bones. After so many years of finding fault with everything about herself, it was little short of miraculous to Bunty, and she never took his adoration for granted.

A blast of frigid air from the hallway announced his arrival home, and Bunty hurried out to greet him. Their eldest boy, Luca, had wide, dark eyes like his mother, and his father's thick dark curls and Mediterranean looks. The child was stamping his feet and leaving chunks of melting snow on the floor with a gleeful grin.

"Look, Mama," he said, holding out a fistful of mistletoe. "Papa said you'd have to kiss us if we brought some home."

Bunty laughed and ran to him, kissing him on his rosy cheek.

"As if you need mistletoe to get me to kiss either of you!" she exclaimed. "But it's very pretty. I shall put a red ribbon on it and hang it up for you."

"Oh, Master Luca, you look chilled through," his nurse said as she bustled into the hallway. "Let's get you in the bath and into clean clothes, quick smart, or you'll not be ready in time for dinner."

For once Luca needed no chivvying, as he'd seen the splendid feast Widdy had been preparing for days now.

"Baby is sleeping, and I'll bring Miss Rose down to say goodnight in a bit, my lady," the efficient Nurse Robinson informed Bunty, with a quick curtsey, before taking Luca's hand and leading him off for his bath.

Bunty turned back to her husband.

"And what about you?" she asked, smiling at him. "Do I need to get you into a hot bath before dinner?"

Ludo returned a pleased grin but shook his head.

"No. Or, at least, in a minute," he said. "I have something for you. Close your eyes."

Bunty laughed and did as he asked, knowing that Ludo would spoil her this Christmas, as he always did. He was forever bringing her presents no matter how often she reassured him she did not need them, but he seemed to enjoy making a fuss of her, and she was hardly going to complain.

"You can open them now."

Bunty gasped at the bouquet of Christmas roses he held out to her, and was at once transported back to their wedding night. He'd decorated his sparse rooms with Christmas roses for her, wanting to make the place welcoming for his new bride.

"Oh," Bunty said, taking them from him with care. "Oh, Ludo, they're so beautiful."

"We found them down near the woods," he said, his blue eyes alight with pleasure at having made her happy. "I'm going to get Mr Widdershins to plant some in the garden, too, outside your parlour. Then you'll have them every Christmas."

Bunty blinked hard and sniffled. Ludo chuckled, pulling her into his arms, careful not to crush the roses.

"Don't cry."

"I'm not crying," she protested, as tears slid down her face.

Ludo touched her cheek and lifted his wet finger for her inspection.

"Proof positive. You're a proper watering pot these past days, anyone would think—"

He closed his mouth with a snap and took a step back, inspecting her.

Bunty huffed. "Oh, and now you've spoiled my surprise. I was going to tell you in the morning."

Ludo gave a crow of triumph and lifted her up into the air, spinning her around as Bunty shrieked. One of the downstairs maids came running to see what the commotion was about, saw them, blushed furiously, and darted away again.

"She's new," Ludo said, grinning. "She's not used to us yet."

Bunty snorted, wondering how she ever looked any of her staff in the eyes. Only the knowledge that they were all wildly jealous let her hold her head up.

"You're sure?" he asked, setting her down gently, one large hand moving to cup her cheek.

"I am," she said, smiling at him.

"How perfect," he said with obvious pleasure. "You are quite perfectly perfect."

Bunty made a sound of incredulity, but he smothered it, kissing her with slow and thorough attention until she remembered they were still standing in the hallway for all to see.

"That's enough," she protested half-heartedly. "Come along. You must get ready. Widdy will have your guts for garters if you make her spoil dinner. Besides which, I have something for you."

"Oh?" he said, waggling his dark eyebrows at her suggestively.

"Not *that*," she said, tsking at him. "There's not time for that though… later."

He sighed heavily, shaking his head with a mournful expression.

"Well, what is it, then? Nothing else will be half so exciting."

Bunty waited until he had closed the bedroom door before setting down her bouquet and handing him the letter which had been burning a hole in her pocket. Ludo stared at it and his eyes met hers.

"Well, open it, then," she said, praying it gave him the news he had been longing for.

Ludo tore open the seal and Bunty held her breath as he read, not daring to breathe until he looked up, his excitement palpable.

"It's from him… from my father. He… he wants to meet me."

Bunty gave a little shout of joy, for she knew what this meant to him. He laughed and pulled her close before turning his attention back to the letter.

"He's been travelling the past few years, which is why we've had such trouble finding him. He says…." Ludo swallowed and tried again. "He says my mother was the love of his life, and he is overjoyed to discover he has a son, and… he can't wait to meet me."

"Oh, Ludo, that's marvellous. I'm so happy for you."

Ludo nodded and set the letter down before tugging her back into his arms. "He says he'll come as soon as the weather improves."

"He'll be so proud of you, love," Bunty said, hugging him. "I know I am."

She watched him as he nodded, believing in himself now in a way he never had when she'd first met him.

"Do you believe in luck or fate?" he asked, frowning a little.

Bunty shrugged. "Perhaps, a little at least, but I think we make our own luck on the whole. Perhaps fate gives us a nudge now and then, but it's what we do with it that counts."

Ludo nodded and reached for one of the roses he'd picked, carefully threading it into her dark hair, behind her ear.

"Everything changed that night in the library. I'd never wanted anything like I wanted you, Bunty, so badly I could taste it. I'd have done anything to get you to marry me. When you practically landed in my lap…." He laughed, shaking his head. "I don't know if it was fate, or luck, but whatever it was I thank my lucky stars, every day, and certainly every night."

"I love you, Ludo," Bunty said, holding him tightly, staring up at him, her own heart echoing everything he had just said.

He touched his finger to the flower in her hair and smiled. "And I you, my own Christmas rose."

Want more Emma?

If you enjoyed this book, please support this indie author and take a moment to leave a few words in a review. *Thank you!*

To be kept informed of special offers and free deals (which I do regularly) follow me on *https://www.bookbub.com/authors/emma-v-leech*

To find out more and to get news and sneak peeks of the first chapter of upcoming works, go to my website and sign up for the newsletter.
http://www.emmavleech.com/

Come and join the fans in my Facebook group for news, info and exciting discussion...
Emmas Book Club

Or Follow me here......
http://viewauthor.at/EmmaVLeechAmazon
Emma's Twitter page

About Me!

    I started this incredible journey way back in 2010 with The Key to Erebus but didn't summon the courage to hit publish until October 2012. For anyone who's done it, you'll know publishing your first title is a terribly scary thing! I still get butterflies on the morning a new title releases but the terror has subsided at least. Now I just live in dread of the day my daughters are old enough to read them.

    The horror! (On both sides I suspect.)

    2017 marked the year that I made my first foray into Historical Romance and the world of the Regency Romance, and my word what a year! I was delighted by the response to this series and can't wait to add more titles. Paranormal Romance readers need not despair however as there is much more to come there too. Writing has become an addiction and as soon as one book is over I'm hugely excited to start the next so you can expect plenty more in the future.

    As many of my works reflect I am greatly influenced by the beautiful French countryside in which I live. I've been here in the South West for the past twenty years though I was born and raised in England. My three gorgeous girls are all bilingual and the youngest who is only six, is showing signs of following in my footsteps after producing *The Lonely Princess* all by herself.

I'm told book two is coming soon ...

She's keeping me on my toes, so I'd better get cracking!

KEEP READING TO DISCOVER MY OTHER BOOKS!

Other Works by Emma V. Leech

(For those of you who have read The French Fae Legend series, please remember that chronologically The Heart of Arima precedes The Dark Prince)

Rogues & Gentlemen

The Rogue

The Earl's Temptation

Scandal's Daughter

The Devil May Care

Nearly Ruining Mr. Russell

Winter's Wild Melody (A Christmas Novella)

One Wicked Winter

To Tame a Savage Heart

Persuading Patience

The Last Man in London

Flaming June

Charity and the Devil

A Slight Indiscretion

The Corinthian Duke

The Regency Romance Mysteries

Girls Who Dare

To Steal A Kiss

To Break the Rules

To Follow Her Heart

To Wager with Love

To Dance with a Devil

To Winter at Wildsyde

To Experiment with Desire

To Ride with the Knight

To Hunt the Hunter

To Dance until Dawn

Daring Daughters

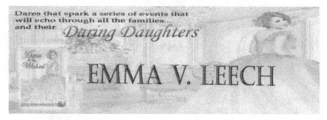

Dare to be Wicked (February 19, 2021)

Dare to be Brazen (tba)

Dare to be Wild (tba)

Stand Alone

The Girl is Not for Christmas (A Regency Christmas)

The Book Lover (a paranormal novella)

Audio Books!

Don't have time to read but still need your romance fix? The wait is over...

By popular demand, get your favourite Emma V Leech Regency Romance books on audio at Audible as performed by the incomparable Philip Battley and Gerard Marzilli. Several titles available and more added each month!

Click the links to choose your favourite and start listening now.

Rogues & Gentlemen

The Rogue ***

The Earl's Tempation

Scandal's Daughter

The Devil May Care

Nearly Ruining Mr Russell

One Wicked Winter ***

To Tame a Savage Heart ***

Persuading Patience

The Last Man in London

Flaming June ***

The Winter Bride, a novella ***

Girls Who Dare

To Dare a Duke

To Steal A Kiss ***

To Break the Rules ***

To Follow her Heart

The Regency Romance Mysteries

Dying for a Duke ***

A Dog in a Doublet **

The Rum and the Fox **

The French Vampire Legend

The Key to Erebus (coming soon)

** Available on Chirp

*** Available on Chirp and Audible/Amazon

Girls Who Dare– The exciting new series from Emma V Leech, the multi-award-winning, Amazon Top 10 romance writer behind the Rogues & Gentlemen series.

Inside every wallflower is the beating heart of a lioness, a passionate individual willing to risk all for their dream, if only they can find the courage to begin. When these overlooked girls make a pact to change their lives, anything can happen.

Eleven girls – Eleven dares in a hat. Twelve stories of passion. Who will dare to risk it all?

To Dare a Duke

Girls Who Dare Book 1

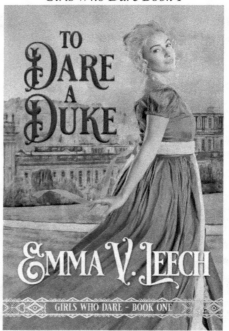

Dreams of true love and happy ever afters

Dreams of love are all well and good, but all Prunella Chuffington-Smythe wants is to publish her novel. Marriage at the price of her independence is something she will not consider. Having tasted success writing under a false name in The Lady's Weekly Review, her alter ego is attaining notoriety and fame and Prue rather likes it.

A Duty that must be endured

Robert Adolphus, The Duke of Bedwin, is in no hurry to marry, he's done it once and repeating that disaster is the last thing he desires. Yet, an heir is a necessary evil for a duke and one he cannot shirk. A dark reputation precedes him though, his first wife may have died young, but the scandals the beautiful, vivacious and spiteful creature supplied the ton have not. A wife must be found. A wife who is neither beautiful or vivacious but sweet and dull, and certain to stay out of trouble.

Dared to do something drastic

The sudden interest of a certain dastardly duke is as bewildering as it is unwelcome. She'll not throw her ambitions aside to marry a scoundrel just as her plans for self-sufficiency and freedom are coming to fruition. Surely showing the man she's not actually the meek little wallflower he is looking for should be enough to put paid to his intentions? When Prue is dared by her friends to do something drastic, it seems the perfect opportunity to kill two birds.

However, Prue cannot help being intrigued by the rogue who has inspired so many of her romances. Ordinarily, he plays the part of handsome rake, set on destroying her plucky heroine. But is he really the villain of the piece this time, or could he be the hero?

Finding out will be dangerous, but it just might inspire her greatest story yet.

To Dare a Duke

From the author of the bestselling **Girls Who Dare Series** – An exciting new series featuring the children of the Girls Who Dare...

The stories of the **Peculiar Ladies Book Club** and their hatful of dares has become legend among their children. When the hat is rediscovered, dusty and forlorn, the remaining dares spark a series of events that will echo through all the families... and their

Daring Daughters

Dare to be Wicked
Daring Daughters Book One

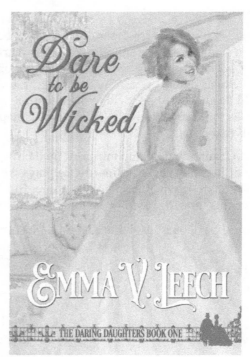

Two daring daughters ...

Lady Elizabeth and Lady Charlotte are the daughters of the Duke and Duchess of Bedwin. Raised by an unconventional mother and an indulgent, if overprotective father, they both strain against the rigid morality of the era.

The fashionable image of a meek, weak young lady, prone to swooning at the least provocation, is one that makes them seethe with frustration.

Their handsome childhood friend ...

Cassius Cadogen, Viscount Oakley, is the only child of the Earl and Countess St Clair. Beloved and indulged, he is popular, gloriously handsome, and a talented artist.

Returning from two years of study in France, his friendship with both sisters becomes strained as jealousy raises its head. A situation not helped by the two mysterious Frenchmen who have accompanied him home.

And simmering sibling rivalry ...

Passion, art, and secrets prove to be a combustible combination, and someone will undoubtedly get burned.

Pre Order your copy here

Dare to be Wicked:

Acknowledgements

Thanks, of course, to my wonderful editor Kezia Cole.

To Victoria Cooper for all your hard work, amazing artwork and above all your unending patience!!! Thank you so much. You are amazing!

To my BFF, PA, personal cheerleader and bringer of chocolate, Varsi Appel, for moral support, confidence boosting and for reading my work more times than I have. I love you loads!

A huge thank you to all of Emma's Book Club members! You guys are the best!

I'm always so happy to hear from you so do email or message me :)

emmavleech@orange.fr

To my husband Pat and my family ... For always being proud of me.

9 782492 133220